DICKINSON'S
Bargain Hunter's Handbook

DICKI

Bargain

David Dickinson

NSON'S

Hunter's Handbook

Your Guide to
the Dos and Don'ts
of Buying Antiques

ORION

The right of David Dickinson to be identified as the author
of this work has been asserted by him in accordance
with the Copyright, Designs and Patents Act 1988.

First published in 2001 by
Orion Books Ltd
Orion House, 5 Upper St Martin's Lane,
London WC2H 9EA

Third impression December 2002

Some of the material in this book was previously published
in *The Antiques Buyer* by David Dickinson published
by Orion Books Ltd in 1999

A CIP catalogue record for this book is available from the
British Library

Printed and bound by Butler & Tanner Ltd,
Frome and London

ISBN 0 75284 145 9

Contents

David's Top Tips

Remember – I may be talking furniture here but most of these tips apply to any antiques.

- *Quality pays.* Try and find the cleanest most honest example of what you want to buy. It's going to cost you a little bit more than the tatty example but in the long run, you will be glad.

- *Buy what you like* – pay no more than you feel you can afford.

- *Ask for the very best price.* Dealers want to do business. Try to negotiate – always ask them what their very best price is.

- *Never over-restore.* Remember, there are degrees of restoration. You can enhance something by restoring it; but, equally, there is a time when you can over-restore and ruin it. If you obey the rule of never buying tat, you won't have this problem.

- With chairs and sofas, *save original covers if you can,* but if they're gone, replace them. No one expects you to sit on stained, worn out rags.

- *Never buy a smiling table.* (Also called yawning tables in the trade.) This is any table with a folding top, such as a card or a games table, a dressing table, a tea table or a sewing box, where the top leaf has warped and no longer sits flat.

- *Highly distressed pieces will distress you.* Avoid them at all costs.

- *Inspection, inspection, inspection, is the name of the game.* At an auction, the goods are on view for perhaps two days. You can go back as many times as you want. Sit back, stand back, weigh it up, think about it, measure it up, go home, have a think about it, bring someone else to have a look. You've got plenty of time. Have a good look.

- *Don't be intimidated; inspect everything thoroughly.* Put your hands on it. Open it up and look inside, look underneath, take out the drawers, look behind. Check signatures, hallmarks, stamp marks. Then get advice.

- *Ask questions.* People won't volunteer information unless you ask them. Generally speaking, they won't tell you lies. Seek as much advice from an expert as you can. Sometimes it's worth paying for that advice – it can save you money in the long run.

- *Study a catalogue carefully.* Read between the lines (what does 'decoration refreshed' really mean?). Always read the small print at the back.

- *Buyer beware* – you, and you alone, are responsible for your mistakes.

- *Get a condition report.* This can be either written or verbal.

- *Get a signed receipt or bill of sale.* Remember that the Trades Description Act is there to protect you.

- *Remember the hidden costs at an auction* – VAT, the buyer's premium and transport home for large items.

- *Be cautious about buying controversial items*, such as lizard-skin suitcases, particularly the ones with a whole head on the top. Even if it's something that's unfashionable at the moment and so you can buy it cheaply, can you use it? Can you sell it? Remember that in the case of something made of animal skin you could end up angering the animal rights people or conservationists.

- *A painted job can hide a hundred sins.* Gilded, lacquered or painted pieces might not be what they seem. Have a look at the quality of the decoration and inspect the carcass inside.

- *Coffee tables are a modern invention.* So-called 'antique' ones are almost always old taller tables that have been cut down, or an old top that has been put on a brand-new base. If it is a marble specimen table, have a careful look at the base – are those stone dolphins old, or are they modern cement? A lot of these are now flooding in from India – made only last week.

- *When buying a collector's watch,* how do you tell the difference between platinum and stainless steel without looking at the hallmark? Check the weight – platinum is very heavy.

- *Always preview the day before at an auction.* Never bid for anything that you have not thoroughly inspected.

- *Always go to a preview in person* – never rely on the catalogue description.

- *Don't get auction fever.* Know your limit and stick to it, but don't lose it for a bid.

- *Never rush to buy.* If the object you are thinking of buying is at an auction, go to the viewing, go away, come back and have another look and see if you still like it enough to bid. If the object you like is in an antiques shop, sleep on it. See how it feels to the refreshed eye. If it is at a fair, go for a stroll, have a cup of coffee and come back before making up your mind.

- *Always check the outbuildings at a big country house sale.* Bargains are often to be found in dark corners away from the madding crowd.

- *Remember that a local connection can send the price up.*

- *Don't be pressurized* into buying.

- *It's in the quality as well as the age.* Appreciate that there is a difference between antiques and second-hand goods.

- *Is it too perfect?* Pristine things are not always what they seem. The chances are they have been very heavily restored, are a fake or a modern copy.

- *Don't buy cracked or repaired ceramics.*

- *Not all antiques are good.* Learn to tell the difference between a trade turn-out or discard and a nice honest piece, fresh to the marketplace.

- *What's underneath that cloth or that brass lamp?* Always lift off an artistically arranged object on top of a piece of furniture you want to buy – it could be hiding a lot of damage, though a little bit of fading is all right. Bubbles in veneer are expensive to iron down.

- *Be ruthless – when in doubt, leave it out.* Some things have had a very tough old life and are only fit for the rubbish bin.

- *Don't buy a worn-out carpet.* At a sale always stay for the turning of the carpets to see what is on the bottom of the pile.

- *Trust your eye.* Buy what you believe in. I have the confidence to do that from years of buying and selling items. Leave room for the unexpected. Always be flexible. Let your eyes and your heart tell you when sometimes you are not sure. Or if acquiring an item means more than the price, if it's special to you, if you've fallen in love with it – buy it.

● *Familiarize yourself with the market-place.* Values and prices change according to the mood and market. A couple of years ago the more decorative items fetched high prices and were fiercely contested; today, people are being that much more careful about what they want to buy. You can use this in your favour if you're buying – Oriental carpets, for example, currently are almost ridiculously cheap. If you're selling such items, hang on until the market goes up.

● *Be prepared to travel for something special.* Look in the trade journals for lists of sales.

● *Avoid a marriage, a liquorice allsort and a cut down.* Stay away from something that has been altered. If it is not what it is supposed to be, it is the kiss of death to buy it. Its value is greatly reduced.

● *The estimate in a sales catalogue is not the selling price – it is only a guideline.*

● *If a piece does not reach its reserve and is 'bought in' (withdrawn from offer), sometimes you can go along later and try to negotiate to buy it privately.* This is often true of large pieces that have travelled long distances to a sale; the vendor will not always want the expense of transporting them home again.

● *Always ask about the provenance* – that is, the history of a piece. Sometimes, when you've bought a piece, you can even research this yourself, thus adding value to whatever it is you have bought.

● *Use your common sense.* If it doesn't look right, it probably isn't. The men who designed the best pieces were excellent craftsmen and designers. You might look at a bookcase and think it looks a bit dumpy. It's obvious to an experienced eye that it's been cut down, but even an inexperienced eye has good, instinctive judgement.

● *Get your eye in by looking,* in as many locations where antique items are displayed as you can – museums, salerooms, antiques shops and fairs. You don't have to buy in order to learn. As you go along learn to make judgements.

● *Recycle what you can't use.* Trade up. Replace with better.

Where and How to Buy

Now we move on to the meat of the matter: actually purchasing a piece. In this chapter I'll cover the places to visit and the ways of buying if you want to remain in control of what is happening. When buying privately, whether it be at an antiques shop, market or fair, it is important to inspect the items you are considering buying carefully. Get your eye in, look at them more than once if you feel like it. Don't rush into making any decisions. And don't worry, we'll get to auctions in due course. There's a whole new world to tell you about there.

We all make mistakes, but by telling you where to buy and what to do when you get there, I hope to save you from some of the pain and the heartache that I have gone through and which hit me in the pocket, because, believe you me, I was very naïve when I first started buying antiques. People were usually very patient and helpful, but I can remember, when I first ventured out into the antiques trade, not even knowing how to haggle in a shop.

Many people feel the same way as I did. They will quite happily go to a boot sale, a Sunday street market or a back-street junk shop, where nothing is very expensive and mistakes won't break the bank, but the idea of venturing into a grander antiques shop or a saleroom feels like making a leap into the unknown. By telling you exactly what to expect and what to look out for as well as explaining the normal procedures I hope to demystify the process of buying antiques, enabling you to become a confident, successful buyer.

It's when you actually purchase an antique that you have to make a decision about its value. Before we set off, let's look at some general issues about spending your money wisely on antiques. (I'll tell you about points relating to different kinds of sales as we go along.)

Rising value

Buying antiques ultimately comes down to a matter of taste. You shouldn't really look at it from a financial point of view, though that obviously is a consideration both because antiques can be very expensive and because they can also appreciate in value over the years. It is a fact that over the last 25 years investment reward on English furniture has far outstripped that on the Stock Exchange. Appreciating in value is part of the appeal of buying antiques.

Looking at antiques from a financial position, I think there are still some very good buys around, particularly in antique furniture, although prices have risen rapidly in the last few years and will continue to do so. When you consider the quality and time-consuming work that's gone into it you will appreciate why in many ways this furniture is impossible to reproduce today. A lot of the raw material, of the wood being used, the veneers, are impossible to get today. It's a bit like fish: certain types of wood have been fished out. Cuban mahogany, for instance, which was famous in the 18th century and used for English brown mahogany furniture, has virtually disappeared. There are substitutes such as Honduras mahogany, but they're not quite the same. The distinctive markings, the grainings and colours of the Cuban were very special, so obviously it is very difficult to reproduce that type of furniture today with exactly that look. Considerations like this are all reflected in the price of a piece.

Getting the best value

The one thing you can say when you have bought a piece of antique furniture today is that at the very moment that you take it away from the auction room or a dealer, the price you have paid was the market price, including perhaps the dealer's profit that he has charged you. Nevertheless, if you decide to go around the corner and sell it five minutes later, you would still retain quite a large proportion of the investment that you have made in it; you won't have lost a great deal of its value.

In my experience over the last 25 years, because of the rising interest in antiques and the resulting scarcity of quality goods, prices are rising. I think I can be quite emphatic and almost guarantee that over the next 10 or 20 years there will be some kind of improvement pricewise in antiques. Though this will always depend very much on trends and fashions: some things have become much more fashionable than other things, while undoubtedly, some things go out of fashion, such as Oriental carpets.

Whether you are hoping to make a profit or simply want to ensure that what you buy doesn't suffer any decrease in value, to be sure of getting good value I suggest you heed the following tips and points.

'Looking at antiques from a **financial** position, I think there are still some very **good** buys around, particularly in antique furniture, although **prices** have risen rapidly in the last few years and will **continue** to do so.'

● **Do your homework**. Take advice, talk to experts and look at two or three similar pieces – after doing all the ground-work, you will be better able to assess prices. Those who jump in at the deep end with a pocket full of money get more than their feet wet.

● **Always buy the best you can afford**. Decide what you can afford, buy the best within that price-range – and stick to it. This applies particularly to collectors. I always think that there's not much point to a collection of tat unless you're a rag-and-bone merchant or a packrat. Remember also that you don't have to fill your house, garden and garage. Some collectors con-tinually buy and sell, trading up, so that they end up with a col-lection of just a few of the best examples, having learned about the items in the process.

If you obey these rules, ten or twenty years down the road your little treasure could also turn out to be your golden goose. Quality is the key – as I shall never tire of repeating, quality will always (barring fads and fashions) increase in value. Whatever you're going out to buy try to buy a really good example.

Take two Worcester cups and saucers, for example. Perhaps one has lived in someone's china cabinet all its life; it is unrubbed, the enamel work is in pristine condition and there are no chips or cracks. It has not been handled, there is no general wear and tear, and it is in superb condition, virtually as the day it was made. Then perhaps in the same sale or shop there is another identical example, at least where model and style are concerned, but there the similarity ends. This second cup and saucer has been used frequently over the past century and a half. It has been washed, it has been rubbed. Perhaps there's a little bit of a chip in the cup, a little bit of a crack in the saucer.

Now the difference between the two when it comes to the price on the day of sale will be considerable – because one is a perfect example and the other is damaged goods. It is rare for things to have survived in such wonderful condition for such a long period, and the pristine cup and saucer are the ones to go for, even if they are ten times more costly because, in my experience, ten years from now the rising value of the mint example will probably have accelerated. From its current price it might have gone up 400 per cent, whereas the value of the cracked example will have gone up, but might have only moved 50 per cent. Not only that; the aesthetic qualities are much better in a good example.

● **Use your common sense**. Once you've satisfied yourself a piece is genuine and decided you want it, you need to apply common sense. Common sense tells you that a shop in Bond Street will nearly always charge more than a shop in the back streets of Birmingham. But common sense will also tell you that an expensive shop would soon go out of business if they were wildly overpriced and didn't give good value for money.

Say you are comparing one shop on the corner at Portobello Market and one in fashionable Chelsea. It doesn't take too much thinking to work out that the Chelsea shop has lovely things in it, but it has reasonably high overheads as well. I wouldn't let something like that deter me because my thinking is, true, the shop in Chelsea will charge that extra amount of money because they've got their rates and so forth but it probably has quite a demanding clientele.

I wouldn't automatically discount the one at the corner of Portobello Market, either, because dealers at the bottom end of the market often find great buys and can afford to sell them on reasonably-priced because their overheads are low. One thing, though, that I would like to stress is that sometimes you can get wonderful deals out of very up-market shops simply because they are used to fine pieces and so do not look on them as out of the ordinary, whereas in a small out-of-the-way shop, that Regency mahogany cabinet might be a real treasure to them, so they will price it high. You weigh up all these considerations when you're making your final decision.

ONCE IN A WHILE

IT'S THE SAME with a dealer as for a private person: once in a blue moon things come before your eyes during your collecting or dealing life that you have to have.

IT'S NOT LIKE buying a car. If a 1985 Mercedes comes along with 20,000 miles – quite rare and a low mileage – and you can't afford it right then, you can let it pass because the chances are there are many others out there just like it that you might buy some day. But when a wonderful piece of art or furniture comes along in a pristine condition or a particular style that tugs at your heart strings, you have only one chance to buy it. It's true that you do see many examples of certain things, but sometimes you know that you'll never see an example exactly like that ever again. You've got to have courage in this business; you've got to chance your arm sometimes because you don't always get second chances. Some wonderful things do come before your eyes and, wrongly or rightly, you have to get off that fence. This is when I say *forget the rules.*

I'VE KNOWN PEOPLE who do outrageous things to acquire an object they have fallen in love with – just as people do outrageous things when they're madly in love. They'll say to me, 'I'll put a deposit on it, I'll find the money somewhere, I'll go and sell something, I'll even sell the wife.' Some people go to extremes to raise money – they'll borrow, get an overdraft, whatever it takes to acquire the object of their dreams. Most of the people I've spoken to for whom this has happened still have their pieces years later. The real kick – the real thrill – is that they acquired whatever it is almost against all odds. It may be worth a great deal more now in financial terms, which is just an added kudos, but they say to me, 'I love it anyway and I'm never going to sell it, however much it is worth.' It is my experience that in most cases when people fall in love with a rare object it is very personal and it is for life. Their marriages may split up but they remain for ever faithful and passionate about their special antique. If you offered them three times the money you couldn't buy it.

Private purchase

Any good antiques dealer will tell you that number one on the list is a private purchase. This is where a private individual invites you to call at his or her home, with a view to selling you a piece of furniture or an object of art. This doesn't happen so much these days because everybody seems to watch antiques programmes on television and as a result now generally send their goods to salerooms; contacting their local antiques dealer is something they used to do. So a rush always goes through me when I hear on the telephone that somebody wishes to sell this or that. I drive to the appointment with happy anticipation and I still get excited when I call at a house to hear the words, 'Oh, Mr Dickinson, we've got this table that's been in the family for 200 years but we're moving house and it's too big for us.'

The item could be almost anything, but the magic words are always 'It's been in the family for…' because then you know that the chances are that you will be looking at a genuine, fresh piece that's been well loved and cared for over many generations. It has never come on to the market and now you've discovered it. It's a little like finding buried treasure.

I'm talking now as an antiques dealer. I'll recognize what I'm looking at and, more importantly, I'll know its worth. I'll tell at a glance whether it's a genuine item, or whether the people are trying to pull the wool over my eyes and have knocked it up out of scrap bits of old wood in the garden shed and cleverly 'antiqued' it – not quite, but you know what I mean! And of course not everyone who is selling a fake knows it. Perhaps the sellers themselves have been fooled when they first bought it and it's my job to break the news to them. Then again, people who have inherited 'Grandma's heirloom table' might not be aware that Grandma bought it brand new in 1935 when she got married. Even so, to them, it's an old and treasured piece of family history and in such cases I decline to buy in a graceful way that won't hurt the seller's feelings.

If the piece is genuine, I will make a fair offer: one that will satisfy the seller and will leave me room for a modest profit when I sell it on. Of course, it's up to them whether they accept my offer or not. For all I know, they might be ringing round all the local dealers to find out the worth of their piece, and they might well end up by sending it to be sold in an auction.

The following true story about buying in a private context, gleefully told to me by a dealer who presented it as something to be proud of, angered me considerably, and I'm afraid it doesn't show up dealers in a good light. Fortunately, such happenings are rare, but there is a lesson to this story.

An old lady came into this dealer's shop and said, 'I need £120 to pay my rates. Will you come to my house and buy some furniture?' He went to her cottage, quickly identified about £900 worth of goods, and said to her, 'Well, that's £100. What else have you got?' She took him into her bedroom and

'If the piece **is** genuine, I will make a fair offer: one that will **satisfy** the seller and will leave **me** room for a modest **profit** when I sell it on.'

he proceeded to identify another £200–£300 worth, for which he gave her £20.

To me, it seems outrageous that the seller has no safeguards when a sale is conducted in a private environment, no recourse against an unscrupulous dealer. I wish I could have advised that lady to put her goods into an auction room, but she probably didn't have the time to wait; sometimes it can take weeks before an auction comes up, there is no guarantee that your goods will sell on the day and even then you still have to wait to be paid.

The moral? If you're determined to sell in this way, never tell a dealer how much you need. Don't let him pick and choose his way through your home, show him just one piece and let him make you an offer. Get at least two valuations before you make your decision.

But to get back to buying. What about you, as a private buyer? How do you get to see private pieces? How do you know if the piece you're there to inspect is genuine and how much to offer for it?

First of all you might see an advertisement in a newspaper or a card in a shop window. Usually, the advertisement will tell you basic information such as dimensions, possibly what it is made from (in the case of wood most people know the difference between pine, oak and mahogany) and how much they want for it. Occasionally the advertisement will say 'offers', in other words, the sellers may be as green as you about the value of their piece and are hoping for an offer that will make them sit up.

Get on the telephone and ask for a detailed description of the table: dimensions such as size and height, shape of legs, any carving, if there are drawers (kitchen tables might have drawers; dining tables do not), materials and approximate age. Ask – if the advertisement hasn't said so – how much they want, then make an appointment to view.

If you have the time, before going to the house, pop into as many local antiques shops as possible to inspect similar tables and ask questions. What is that table made from? How much

BUYING FROM A FRIEND

ONE RATHER DIFFICULT AREA I am often asked about is what you should do if you are buying an antique from a relative or a good friend. You want to be scrupulously fair and the piece is valuable, but how do you go about it? First, you should ask for a valuation from a dealer and stick to that price. It will cost you a few pounds in the valuer's fee but will save any possible bad feeling later. You should also ask the valuer to give a condition report (see page 55) and attach this to your receipt, which the vendor should sign. You might say you don't need a receipt between friends, but where money is concerned, you should always be business-like; and it is certainly a helpful document to make use of, regardless of whether the vendor is a friend or not.

more would it be worth if it had two leaves, or four? What price range do such tables fall into? You can also look in books about antiques. Books can only show a few examples; they can never let you get your hands on the object to feel the wood, and the values are nearly always out of date or guesstimates. However, a good book can give you a rough idea of the difference between shapes and styles, such as a pedestal leg or a cabriole leg and a claw foot or a pad foot.

When you arrive at the house and they show you the table, the first thing you should do is to measure it, to reassure yourself that it will fit in your dining room. It is amazing the number of people who, when asked for dimensions over the telephone, give a rough estimate that is usually wrong.

You will know at once if this table you're now inspecting 'looks right'. If it has a table cloth and ornaments on it, ask the seller to take everything off so that you can have a proper look. If it is stuck in a corner of the hall where there is no light, ask if you can carry it into a room with a better light. Then remembering what I've said about common sense and using your eyes, not to mention your very fresh look at a few genuine antique tables, see if the table still looks right. Get on your hands and knees, and look under the table. Tip it over if it's light enough and look at the colour of the carcass. Does it look raw and new? Are there shiny new screws? Are there brackets holding the legs on (a sure sign of serious structural damage)? Can you see where new stain has been slapped on, indicating that the piece is fake or has been extensively rebuilt?

If all looks well to your sensible, albeit untrained eye, discuss the price. You should have some idea of what this size and type of table will be worth because of your initial research. At this stage you might well fall into a moral dilemma. Suppose similar tables you have seen in antiques shops cost anything up to £6,000 and these people naïvely are asking just £150: what should you do? In my case, as a dealer, I am usually called in to make an offer or to value goods, so I have a professional duty to be fair and a reputation to maintain; but a private buyer does not have that duty or reputation. I can't tell you what to do – that has to be up to you. Whatever you offer, it is also up to the seller to protect himself. Just as you have taken the trouble to do your homework, he should have done the same. But I would always advise you to be fair. What goes around comes around.

Get a receipt

You want to buy the table and you've agreed a price – but remember that the principle governing the law is 'buyer beware' (see Sale of Goods Act 1979, page 23). 'Buyer beware' is a legal term that means exactly what it says. By law you are responsible for your decision to purchase or not – the risk is on your side. If you're not yet such an expert that you know exactly what it is that you're buying, you can safeguard yourself a little: always ask for a detailed receipt.

In the example of your private purchase of a table, ask the owners to write on a piece of paper what they have told you over the telephone or in person. They might not know the style, the date, or the type of wood, but they could say: 'A 3.5m (9ft) table, believed to have been in the family for over

100 years, of a solid reddish-brown wood believed to be mahogany with square legs and three leaves.' Get the owners to date and sign it. If the table proves to be made in 1960 and made of plywood, in principle you have some redress and can ask for your money back. This applies to anything that you buy, whether Clarice Cliff 'Bizarre' pottery, a picture or a sideboard.

An additional reason for asking for a receipt is to prove that you own the antique you have just purchased. If you pay for it by cash without a receipt, and it is amazing the number of things that change hands this way, how can you prove, should the occasion ever arise, that you paid for it? Sometimes antiques have been known to have been stolen; in order to prove that you paid for it, get that receipt. It may also be useful for insurance purposes, when you have to decide how much to value a piece for. Your insurance company will also require a receipt in the case of a claim.

A receipt – also known as a bill of sale – can also protect you. Under the Trades Description Act you cannot be misled – and

'**Sometimes** antiques have been known to have been **stolen**; in order to prove that you paid for it, get that **receipt**.'

if you are, the perpetrator can be guilty of a serious offence. If you were to come to me and say, 'I would like to buy that bookcase, Mr Dickinson, please would you tell me about it?' I'd say, 'Well, it's definitely Continental, possibly Swedish, 19th century, probably circa 1890 to 1900 (circa meaning 'round about'). It's in good, original condition, with its original, untouched gilding. We've cleaned it. There have been some little knocks and chips so we have done some light restoration to it. I'm prepared to sell it to you for – ' and then we would start to negotiate, after which I would put that agreed price down on your receipt, together with something like: 'In good original condition, circa 1890 – Continental – walnut and gilt.'

When you went away you would have something in your hand that would tell you exactly what you had and would be legally binding. If at some stage in the future it turned out not to be what I said it was, if it turned out to be 1950s and was faked to look old or heavily restored, you could come back to me and say, 'This was total misrepresentation. I want my money back.'

The situation is a little different in a saleroom or an auction. There it is very much a case of buyer beware (see page 62).

Buyer's rights

The following points should not be taken as the definitive guide to consumer law. I hope they will give you pointers to what your rights in normal circumstances cover. It doesn't matter if you buy from an individual, a shop, fair, market or auction, these rights still apply. These are your statutory rights and cannot be withdrawn from you by any small print in catalogues or receipts or 'terms of business'

1. GENERAL

It must be emphasised that the buyer can only effectively exercise any available right
a) if he can find the seller after the purchase of any item has been completed; and

b) if the seller is of sufficient financial means to return the purchase price and/or compensate the buyer

This is one very good reason for buying from a reputable dealer. The buyer is most unlikely to be able to trace a seller from a car boot sale.

If buying from an agent e.g. a dealer selling on behalf of a private seller, then any claim will only be against the private seller and not the agent, unless the agent has failed to make clear that he is acting as agent

When buying any item, ask for a receipt which gives the

a) date of purchase;

b) purchase price;

c) full description of the item being purchased; and

d) name and address of the seller

2. IMPLIED INTO AN AGREEMENT WHEN YOU BUY

If the seller is selling privately or in the course of a business

a) That the seller owns what he is selling (a condition). Note that if a stolen item is bought, the buyer will not obtain title to that item. If it is claimed by the original owner, then it will have to be returned to that original owner. The buyer's only recourse is against the seller for the return of the purchase price together with any other foreseeable losses.

S.12 (1) SALE OF GOODS ACT 1979

b) (Unless anything is said to the contrary) that the item being bought is free from incumbrances e.g. not subject to any form of finance agreement (a warranty). However, if the item is a vehicle and bought by a private buyer, in good faith, without notice of that finance agreement, then the buyer will obtain the vehicle free of the finance agreement.

S.12 (2) SALE OF GOODS ACT 1979   S27 HIRE-PURCHASE ACT 1964

c) That the item being bought will correspond with its description (a condition)   S.13(1) SALE OF GOODS ACT 1979

If the seller is selling in the course of a business

That the item is of satisfactory quality (a condition). What this means is that a reasonable person would regard it as being of satisfactory quality after taking into account i) the description of the item, ii) its price, iii) its appearance and finish, iv) its freedom from minor defects, v) its safety, vi) its durability, and/or vii) its fitness for the purpose for which an item of the kind in question is commonly supplied. However, a) if what makes the item unsatisfactory is either drawn to the buyer's attention before the contract is made or b) the buyer has a full opportunity to examine and the examination would have revealed the defect, then the buyer cannot claim that that defect makes the item unsatisfactory.

S.14(2) SALE OF GOODS ACT 1979

3. Misrepresentations

If the buyer is told something by the seller which has the object and result of persuading the buyer to buy the item and what the buyer has been told is false, then the seller has made a misrepresentation. On finding out about the misrepresentation, the buyer has a choice of either rescinding the contract, i.e. giving back the item and recovering the purchase price, or receiving compensation. This applies whether the misrepresentation was made by the seller fraudulently or innocently.

SECTIONS 1 AND 2 MISREPRESENTATION ACT 1967

4. Excluding liability

As long as the buyer is acting as a private consumer, the seller cannot exclude or restrict his liability.

5. Remedies

If the breach is a breach of condition or misrepresentation, the buyer is entitled to his or her money back on return of the item together with any other foreseeable loss, e.g. travel costs. If the breach is a breach of warranty, then normally the only entitlement is to compensation for the loss suffered, e.g. if the item is subject to a finance agreement, then the cost of paying off that finance agreement.

6. ENFORCING THE REMEDY

If the seller will not voluntarily compensate the buyer or take back the item, then the only remedy might be to take court proceedings against the seller. Before doing this the buyer must give the seller every opportunity to compensate the buyer for his or her loss. The buyer should write to the seller, keeping a copy of the letter, setting out why he has a claim, what is wrong with the item and what the buyer wants, e.g. money back. If the buyer has any document supplied by the seller on making the purchase (e.g. the receipt referred to above), then he should send a copy. If the buyer has been told by an expert that the description of the item is not correct, then that should be embodied in a written report and a copy sent to the seller. The buyer should make clear what he is looking for by way of compensation and that the letter will be referred to at any court hearing on the question of costs. Legal advice should be considered if the loss is likely to be substantial.

Antiques shops

Much more likely than a private purchase is that you'll buy in an antiques shop. While we're on the subject, let me digress a little and tell you the story of my own.

I had known Chris Haworth since my first day at school. Our friendship continued through into our marriages. Lorne and I and Chris and his wife used to go to each other's homes for dinner or just drop in for a chat. Like me, Chris was interested in antiques and collected a bit, although he didn't buy and sell as I did. One day, out of the blue, when the four of us were together, Chris and I suddenly decided we should have a go at running our own business. It was an enormous step. Chris was making a good living as a fleet car manager for a major automobile company and he'd be giving up the security of that to open up a shop and stock it in the hope that we could attract customers and make it work. But Chris's character complemented mine; we were two sides of one coin. I was the more flamboyant, gregarious type while he was steady and more

CARLTON HOBBS

I'm a great admirer of a very stylish firm in Pimlico owned by two young men my age: the Hobbs brothers, Carlton and John. To my eyes they are some of the leading lights of the antiques business in this country today. They have risen to the pinnacle by stocking the most exquisite, extraordinary and expensive items. If you're a highly discerning collector, a Rothschild or a international movie star or an interior decorator who wants to knock a client's socks off, then you'd go there. These are men who in the last 25 years have become prominent because of their eye and ability to acquire the most dramatic and superb pieces. There are several places you would go to in the world for the exotic and extraordinary: a certain dealer in Paris, one in Rome, but when in London it would have to be Carlton Hobbs.

cautious, working quietly away in the background. Many people have thought I was the more outgoing partner, but we had a partnership of equals. Back then, when we were both so new and green in the business I don't think either of us could have done it without the support of the other.

Encouraged by our wives, we put in about £1,500 each to buy and stock a little shop in the centre of Disley. I was travelling with Lorne at the time as her manager and was home for just a couple of weeks at a time, but Chris ran the business full time. At first, before we could afford an assistant, this was a problem because one of us would have to go out on the road buying, while the other was running the shop.

Simple things we hadn't taken into account, like how to value, how to price up our pieces, were just hit and miss until we became more experienced. We'd take turns to look after the shop and go out on the road, our wives helped with cleaning and dusting – we all pitched in. It was an enormous jump into the unknown, but we didn't think we were doing anything that remarkable. I know that many would-be antiques dealers will be very cheered by my modest beginning – it shows that the sky's the limit if you have confidence.

JACK DONOVAN

In Portobello Road there used to be a man with a small shop crammed with the most extraordinary toys, wonderful automatons. One of the biggest collectors of automata in the world was Prince Rainier of Monaco. Jack Donovan was known as the King of Toys. The door to his wonderland was never left open: you'd have to knock. A face would appear, and if he half liked the look of you he'd let you in. (Some of the more eccentric dealers would never let you in. I could never figure out how they did any business.) As a young guy I'd say politely, 'Mr Donovan, please may I come in and have a look at some of your pieces?' He'd show me, talking me through his rare collection. What were toys in the 19th century can go for £50,000 today.

Most of Jack Donovan's collection was not for sale. He'd sell some lesser pieces in order to survive, but he was an example of a dealer who in his heart is a collector, someone who can't bear to let many of his things go. You can still be a dealer and build up a collection by keeping certain things back. I try not to do that, but one day I might wake up and think to myself, 'No, I cannot and will not sell that,' and then I'll know that I have caught the bug.

In fact, we had remarkable confidence. A little back-street junk shop filled with cheap bits and bobs was not for us. We wanted the best, right from the start, even if we were stretching our resources to the limit and beyond. We wanted the spotlights in the shop window and Bond Street glamour. Not for us an ad in the local paper – we wanted the glossy advertisement in the best position in a trade magazine, the one the top dealers and collectors subscribed to – and the approach paid off.

One day a Swedish lawyer based in Disley, who used to buy regularly from us, mentioned that he had contacts in Sweden who were very interested in antiques. When he said that he would tell them about our shop and the nice things we had, I don't think we paid much attention. One day the lawyer turned up at the shop with a tiny man, about 1.5 metres (5 feet) tall, dressed in a cowboy's regalia – the Stetson, the shirt, the bolo string tie, the jeans, the cowboy boots. This elf spoke very little

English, but speaking through the lawyer he said he was very impressed with the stock. Eventually, after inspecting every piece, he asked, 'How much?'

I said, 'How much for what?'

'All of it!' he replied.

Chris and I were stunned. We just looked at each other, too amazed to speak. Eventually we decided we would simply open up our stock books, show him what every item had cost us and ask for a straight 17.5 per cent profit on top of that. He agreed – and we sold him the whole stock. There were about five or six other antiques shops in Disley and word sped around the village that Dickie and his pal had got a millionaire 'Texan'. Everyone flocked by to get an eyeful of this phenomenon, but he didn't buy from anyone else.

This 'cowboy' turned out to be one of the wealthiest men in Sweden. His name was Bent Erlanson, known to his friends as Little Bent. I didn't know at that stage that he was a multi-millionaire entrepreneur and ombudsman who was fascinated by cowboys, going every year to the Tucson Round-up in Arizona. Apart from many commercial interests he also had a Disneyland type of ranch in Sweden that he had named the Ponderosa, like the TV series. After cleaning us out, he invited us to visit him in Sweden. We went and discovered that the reason he had bought all our antiques was to supply the shops in his Western-style holiday camp environment – a Butlin's for cowboys, with shoot-outs in the street and Wild West shows.

Little Bent came once more to Disley with three other Swedish businessmen, all major players in their own areas: one was the marzipan king of Sweden; another was the burger king of Sweden and the last one was the frozen food king of Sweden. Between them, they bought up the shop again.

Things went so well that eventually Chris and I got up to about £90,000 turnover. In those days there was stock relief, which meant that you could invest your profits without paying tax back into the company. With me having eyes bigger than my belly, it wasn't long before we focused our sights on the Mayfair of Cheshire – Wilmslow. We had warnings from many people that it was all frock and no knickers there, but I wouldn't be told. Selling our shop in Disley at a handsome profit, in 1980 off we went to open a glamorous emporium in the centre of Wilmslow at a hefty rent, since we couldn't find anywhere to buy. But business was never good and a recession was looming. Three years later, Chris and I amicably decided to split up and go in different directions – remaining the best of friends until he died.

After Chris and I closed that business down, I considered opening on my own in Manchester. I did my sums, totted up my capital, and was rather nervous at the high overheads, more than anything I had incurred before. But then I remembered Imad Al-Midani, whom I had first met when he bought some of the finest pieces from the Wilmslow shop. I asked Imad if he would like a silent interest in the business, to which he readily agreed.

Imad was the most generous, gentlemanly person I had ever met. Even though he had been brought up in a fabulously wealthy family, educated at the American School in Beirut and completed his education in England, he was very modest and charming. I remember once when we and our wives went to stay at the Dorchester for the weekend, even though his father was a main shareholder of the Park Lane hotel, Imad was the kind of man who, when we came down for dinner in the evening and the maitre d' came rushing across, courteously insisted that we were not given priority over existing customers, but would be seated only when convenient. And even though he was a partner in the business he insisted on paying the full price with mark-up for every piece I sold him to furnish his wonderful country mansion. The business thrived for a few years. But this antiques business is not all go, go, go: things can get very tough. When another recession hit the country seven years later in 1991, at the same time as the tripling of my rent, I decided to dissolve my partnership with Imad and close the shop. I started to concentrate on fairs, something that I had already been doing successfully for some years, and now I make a good living by buying carefully and doing two or three fairs a year.

Buying in an antiques shop means, of course, that you're going to encounter an antiques dealer. Now before you say it, let me say it. Antiques dealers are untrustworthy rogues and sharp practice is the norm – or at least many people seem to think so. I don't agree. It would be naïve of me to say that these individuals don't exist – they do. Like all businesses, it takes all types. Above all avoid the likes of dear old Auntie Wainwright, the shrewd junk-shop owner in the beguiling television series, *The Last of the Summer Wine*. The Auntie Wainwrights of this world have the knack of luring innocent customers into their shops and selling them fools' gold, something they didn't want, often at hugely inflated prices, and before you know it, you're out of their shop, invoiceless and clutching some piece of rubbish.

'Antiques dealers are **untrustworthy rogues** and sharp practice is **the norm** – or at least many people seem to think so. I **don't** agree.'

In fact there are fewer problems, believe it or not, in buying from an established and reputable antiques dealer, inasmuch as you are dealing with someone who has a good reputation to protect and they want to keep that good reputation. True, you have to negotiate a price with them and it's up to you to decide if the price is a fair one; but at the end of the day, that dealer has to give you a bill of sale. He has to describe on that piece of paper what he has sold you and, depending on how persistent you are, you can ask for a huge amount of detail to be included. This piece of paper can protect you (see page 21).

But I'm pleased to say, that in my experience, the vast majority are good dealers. Over the years I've met and dealt with thousands. They have been a mixture of hard-working professionals and some of the most wonderful characters that one could possibly hope to meet.

Trade societies

Many of the major dealers belong to societies, such as the British Antique Dealers' Association (BADA), which I belong to, or the London and Provincial Antique Dealers' Association (LAPADA), both of which are highly respected. There are many criteria to joining such organizations. First of all, you are invited to join: you don't apply. They have codes of practice and regulate their members as a lot of professional bodies do. Membership of one of these societies is not a 100 per cent guarantee of a dealer's integrity, but a dealer being a member of a society that has rules, regulations and codes of ethics is a good indication. However, I would not want to say that someone who is not a member of a society is not a good dealer, because there are many who choose not to join. I was approached many times to join BADA, recommended by other members, and I did not join immediately. I thought long and hard and finally I did join because it is so well-regarded throughout the world; my feelings were that being a member would be helpful to give confidence to my international clients. Also, there are many things you can go to the society for, such as legal advice, advice on shipping, regulations and so forth.

BADA and LAPADA both have their own fairs in London once a year: BADA has the Grosvenor House Fair and the BADA Fair on the King's Road; LAPADA has one at the Commonwealth Institute in Kensington and also a show at the National Exhibition Centre in Birmingham.

Where are the best dealers?

Many of the best-quality dealers are in London. An example of someone with an eye for the extraordinary is Guinevere in the King's Road, a French lady who has been there for many years and gained a first-class reputation for decorative antiques. When she first opened her shop in the New King's Road she was perhaps one of only a few people in what was considered then an unfashionable part of the road; now 50 shops have gathered around her like moths around a flame.

There are of course the establishment firms on Bond Street, such as Partridges for some English but mostly grand Continental furniture; and Mallets, supplier of English furniture in early walnut – very much the absolute top-of-the tree retail house. In Pimlico Road a group of designer quality antiques businesses has grown up with a whole new look – it's stylish and it's hip. The Fulham Road is now a secondary Bond Street in many ways, with a collection of top-drawer English furniture dealers, and Westbourne Grove is getting to be a hub of commercial dealers.

In the country there are many established antiques dynasties, run by the same family for several generations. These demonstrate that the very best of everything is not only to be found in the West End of London: it can also be found elsewhere, in established country firms which have been working for many years in places such as Harrogate and Bath. (In recent years Bath has dried up a little, but nevertheless, it's a great hunting ground with lots of shops).The Cotswolds are perhaps the richest hunting ground in the country, though they are declining a bit from a dealer's point of view. There was a time 15 or 20 years ago when the Cotswolds were at their peak. A lot of travelling dealers from all over the world used to go there; but by and large they've moved on, like a shoal of herrings to new feeding grounds, perhaps leaving more space for the modest private antiques hunters to browse.

Fairs and markets

Many people are wary of this type of bazaar-like venue because they think they're filled with rogues, tinkers and snake-oil charlatans. But such places do have merits and advantages. To me these are the most interesting and the most fun because you never know what you'll find. However, by their very nature, these venues can be quite casual, and, unless you're going to an established and fairly grand fair, such as those at the NEC in Birmingham, or at Olympia or the Grosvenor House Hotel in London, where the dealers are carefully vetted, often it really is a case of 'buyer beware': it's all very well getting a nice guarantee or bill of sale, but that's no use to you if the seller does a runner and you never see them again. But there are many different types of venues and some are better than others.

● **Car boot sales**. Bottom of the pile are the informal and local car boot sales increasingly being held up and down the country, where you can buy almost anything from second-hand clothes to garden plants. You can also buy the odd genuine antique, and, if you're very lucky, you might even buy a frippery for a couple of pounds that turns out to be Fabergé and worth £10,000. It is the thrill of the unexpected that keeps people going to car boot sales, although for a serious antique hunter looking for a particular item, I would never recommend them since you might have to go to dozens and still not find what you are looking for. The biggest drawback to these smaller markets is that you can buy a load of rubbish on the spur of the moment; the plus side is that nothing ever costs very much so if you later decide you've made a mistake, you won't be too much out of pocket.

'You can also buy the odd **genuine** antique, and, if you're very **lucky**, you might even buy a **frippery** for a couple of pounds that turns out to be **Fabergé** and worth £10,000.'

● **Open-air or flea markets.** These are next up the scale. There are the summer ones, such as those you can find in huge fields, showgrounds or cattle markets, some of which are milestone events in the calendar with several thousand stallholders congregating there to sell their wares. Established flea markets are held regularly, weekly and even daily, such as the one in the centre of Paris.

If you want to branch out and be adventurous on holiday you can find them through guide books or your travel agent, though remember that, whatever you buy, you have to carry back with you. On one occasion when I was quite new to the antiques game, Lorne and I were in Spain, and I spotted a large terracotta figure of a man for sale. It was German and had spent most of its life in a castle high in the Pyrenées. For some reason, I took a fancy to it. We had our small Jaguar E-type and on to the roof rack went this life-size object. Driving it home was quite nerve-racking, as we jolted down mountain roads, over potholes and around sharp bends. At any moment I expected shards of terra-cotta to shower down around us, but the figure survived and arrived home without a crack. Embolded by this, in Italy we bought faience and majolica pieces, in Portugal, earthenware pans and pots – we used to drag back some strange and exotic bits and pieces, all strapped on to that roof rack.

If you are prepared to take a chance that what you are buying is genuine, because I doubt if you'll ever be able to get a refund from a flea market held in a field near Budapest, and you have the space in your luggage or in your car, then you can get some very striking pieces from as far afield as Russia or East Germany, where a new market in antiques has opened wide. In those areas money is in such short supply that many people are having to sell family heirlooms for tragically small sums. If you're lucky, and can overcome the language problem, you can buy historic pieces, such as lost treasures of the Romanov period, or early Communist memorabilia, which are increasingly collectable. However, I cannot put my hand on my heart and say, yes, buy this or that, because those are specialist fields and you need to be an expert to be sure of what you're getting. There are very few books available in English for research and the value of antiques from Russia, Poland and other former Communist countries is still a largely unknown territory.

● **Emporiums**. These are places where, at a single location, such as a mall or an arcade, a large warehouse or a street market, a permanent group of dealers display their wares. Usually, their space is very small and for that reason most of them specialize in smaller objects, whether furniture, decorative items, silver and jewellery or collector's items, from comics to books to toys. If you are looking for something particular or something to add to your collection in a friendly atmosphere, this is the kind of place to go.

For example, in Bermondsey, London, you can find a street market early every Friday morning, jam-packed with stallholders selling the most eclectic range of articles. You will often find 'the trade' here, dealers who perhaps own rather grand shops, looking for bargains. If they can bargain and find good deals so can you, but you must get there early before the tourists arrive. Remember that as these stallholders have to unpack and then pack up everything they don't sell, they'd far rather sell to you than take it all back to the lock-up where they store it. Most major towns have similar markets or emporiums.

It is worth pointing out that because the stall- or booth-holders are permanent or regulars, they are not normally fly-by-nights who will con you, take your money and do a runner. All the same always remember to get a proper receipt with an address and phone number where you can contact them later if necessary.

● **Antiques fairs**. These are at the top end of the scale. Many of them might look grand because often the venues are grand (such as the Grosvenor House Hotel in Mayfair where the top 100 crème de la crème dealers set out their exquisite wares) but don't be put off. If you go to a big antiques fair there will be a large collection of dealers displaying their wares to the best of their advantage in an open market-place environment. It might be rather swish, with stands and curtains, but it is still a market-place and they are there to sell. You are there to look and possibly buy in your own time, when you are ready.

Not everything for sale is expensive. Goods on sale at places like Grosvenor House are so appealing that at the end of the first day (when some say in excess of £100 million changes hands) stocks have to be replenished.

All kinds come on the stands. Some of them are incredibly wealthy, people who can count their fortune in billions. But I want to say to all of you who make more modest livings that even though there are a lot of glamorous, expensive items to be had, I and all the other hard-working dealers also sell much more modest pieces. I'm only too happy to spend time with anybody from any walk of life in any price range. Prices have risen considerably, but I still think you can find very nice small pieces of furniture or decorative items from about £500 and go from there. It is possible to find a nice single 19th-century carved chair within that price range, for instance, or a lovely mirror that will grace your home; you won't always get an oil but you can get a magnificent signed watercolour. The other day I bought a delightful little Italian picture frame in perfect condition, inlaid with shells, that will sell for about £400. There are lots of nice things you can buy even at the most rarefied shows. The range of objects might surprise you.

What you can depend on at these fairs is quality. At fairs of this standard because you will get a properly headed bill of sale with a full description of what you have bought so you can always contact the dealer at his shop or home base and get your money back.

Speaking for myself, in the months leading up to a big fair I am digging very deep, searching all over the country for things of quality, desirable items that I believe to be valuable and that customers will want. I'm always looking for something that's just a little different or exotic because there will be 400 competitors at the fair.

Knowing what my customers want comes from years of experience in the trade, of selling antiques to the public and having a very good eye. I'm not just buying something commercial (that is, something that is readily saleable); I'm buying what I believe in. I have the confidence to do this from years of buying and selling items. I have found that if I buy what I believe in and really like, I can talk to potential customers with genuine honesty and passion. It makes life easier for me, because when I like something I'm excited about it, and I can transfer that excitement to my clients because it's from the heart. I have a feeling that people 'suss' you out very quickly when you talk in half-muted tones about something that you don't have a genuine regard for. If you don't like a piece, why should they?

From years of being reliable I have built up a solid base of clients who trust me. I'm telling you this because when you go to a reputable fair you will learn by looking at the very best, genuine articles and a novice can distil years of the joint experience of dozens of dealers if he or she looks, learns, listens and asks the right questions – you will almost always buy a piece that is what it is supposed to be.

● **Ask questions**. If you see something you like, ask as many questions as you like, just as you did when you were getting your eye in. Don't be shy. There's nothing like a bit of flattery. People, including me, like to be told that the pieces they are exhibiting are lovely. If you go on to someone's stand and say, 'Can I have a look at your rubbish?' you'll have an appropriate

'The other day I bought a **delightful** little Italian picture frame in **perfect** condition, inlaid with shells, that will sell for about **£400**.'

reaction. At one show, a really obnoxious bumptious type walked on to a neighbouring stand run by a friend of mine. With his neighing haw-haw voice, it was, 'What is this laddy? What is that, hmm?'

My chum said, 'Oh, that's a Regency curtain pole.'

'Hmm' said Mr Bumptious. 'Tell me about it, laddy – go on laddy, what is it?'

'Well, sir, it's wonderfully carved, it has these original brass bits – '

'Any provenance, hmm? Any provenance, laddy?'

Losing patience my chum said, 'As matter of fact, sir, there is a provenance. I bought it off the back of a K-reg Volvo in a car park on the M6.' Mr Bumptious slunk off and wasn't seen in that part of the fair again.

So go about with a little bit of cunning, use a little bit of tact and charm, and you'll find the dealers eating out of your hand.

At the same time, tell the dealer frankly that you will be looking at other alternatives. Don't say it in such a way that it comes out like a threat, just make it honest. 'I'm going to look at several spoon-backed chairs. Within the next twenty-four hours I'm going to make my mind up and buy one.' In other words someone is going to get your hard-earned money – and it's a question of who. If the dealer wants your money he's going to work for it by telling you all you want to know about that chair and by offering to knock a bit off. Tell him you will want a proper receipt and a guarantee. If a dealer is snooty and refuses to do any of these things, be strict with yourself and walk away. It makes no difference whether you've come to a large open-air market with hundreds of other stands, such as the famous Newark sale, or to a town where there are plenty of other antiques shops stuffed with a large variety of goods from which you will be able to make an informed choice. There are plenty of competitors out there who will be very happy to sell to you.

A lot of people are nervous about following this advice. They are scared of being a nuisance, or of looking silly. But there is an easy way of going about it. Politeness is a great winding sheet. 'Would you do this – could you show me that, could you turn it upside down? I don't know what I'm looking for yet, but I'm hoping you'll show me what you have. I want to have a really good look at this chair.' If you charm the dealer he is more than likely to let you have a jolly good look, and point out a few faults if there are any and offer you advice. Genuine dealers will go out of their way not to rook you but to help you – after all, they want your custom and they hope you might come back year after year.

Some of my best customers have wandered on to my stand looking as if they didn't have a penny to their name. A few years ago at Olympia an old man with tanned, wrinkled skin came toddling by in a bright blue jacket with brass buttons and a little white cap with braid on it. I don't know why, but I nodded and said, 'Good morning, Captain.' I didn't know that he actually owned a yacht, as well as a fleet of tankers. He nodded back and stepped on to my stand. He looked a little weary, so I invited him to sit, which he did, while I got on with chatting to another client. The 'Captain' turned out to be a Greek shipping tycoon, who brought some beautiful pieces from me that day, perhaps because I didn't pressure him. When he had chosen several pieces and departed, I had to run after him with the invoice. 'Excuse me, who are you?' I asked. 'How will you pay?' His secretary looked astonished, as if to say you must be the only person here today who doesn't know John Latsis, billionaire! He bought many more pieces from me over the years.

I was at a fair once in Birmingham when a lady I can only describe as being a Margaret Rutherford character came on to the stand – in fact I thought it *was* Margaret Rutherford. She was quite heavy in posture with the Rutherford tweeds, large pull-down squashy hat, heavy lisle-type stockings wrinkled and buckled as though she was wearing two or three pairs, and a plastic shopping bag. She was quite eccentric; you almost could see her in the *VIPs* with Elizabeth Taylor and Richard Burton in the scene at the airport where someone says to the old bat, 'I can't find you on the check-in list' and suddenly a supervisor comes up and says, 'Good afternoon, your Grace – she's in first class.'

Anyway, on the stand were a very fine quartetto of delicate Sheraton tables, dated about 1780, in a nest from which they could all slide out. 'Miss Rutherford' stomped up to these tables and began to drag them out quite roughly. I could see their long fragile legs about to break so I said, 'Excuse me, madam, may I help you?' I slid them out gently and let her have a good look. In her deep voice she asked how much they were. £5,700, I informed her. She rumbled, 'Mmm, hmm, hmm,' then left. She came back four or five times. Each time, I nodded at her, 'Nice to see you, madam.' Each time, she dragged at the tables – in fact, she was doing exactly what I have told you to do: inspect, inspect, inspect, go away and come back again; but I would hope you would treat the items with more care. 'Let me assist you,' I would say, coming forward and gently taking the tables from her clumsy hands. In my mind I was thinking, 'She's going to smash these tables, she's not going to buy them and soon they'll be matchwood.' But nevertheless I persevered and was polite because that's what you're there for and really, she wasn't a bad old sort.

I almost reeled into the tables with shock when on the final visit she said. 'Well, I suppose you'll take £5,500 for them?' Recovering quickly, I said 'I would indeed.' She signed a cheque and after she left someone came across to me and said. 'Do you know who that is?' I had to confess that I did not. She was one of the richest women in Warwickshire. Every year she'd come to this fair and buy something of really superior quality. That year, I was the lucky lad who was chosen. If I had been impatient with her and told her to clear off, to leave my tables alone before she broke them, I would not have been chosen. Which just goes to show.

● **Don't be pressurized**. This is a golden rule in any buying situation. Many people prefer to wander around a fair or market because they are somewhat intimidated when they go to a shop and have to ring a bell. At a fair there's no door bell and no coercion from sales staff. If you are someone with less confidence, remember that you can walk from stand to stand without obligation and if anyone puts any pressure on you before you are ready, you can simply walk off. A good dealer won't try to intimidate you. If a dealer does try to twist your arm, whatever happens, don't be pushed into making a decision on the spot. Go away, look for other similar pieces, compare them, then come back. If you miss it, you miss it; there'll always be another piece, possibly a nicer one – that's the thrill of the antiques' hunt.

At a fair there is a lively atmosphere with healthy competition – competition that can work for you as well as against you. Anything up to 30,000 people attend the bigger fairs, so if you spot something that appeals to you don't wait too long to make an offer. On the other hand, depending on the size and the grandeur of the fair, the dealers have often paid a great deal of money to be there for that day or that week, from the rent of

'If you **miss** it, you miss it; there'll always be **another** piece, possibly a nicer one – that's the **thrill** of the antiques' hunt.'

their stand to such overheads as accommodation, transport and insurance, and they are anxious to sell.

● **Ask for the very best price.** Suppose you have seen something on a particular stand that appeals to your eye. You have asked all the right questions and the dealer has said he will give you a detailed receipt. If that piece is still there when you go back, you can say, 'I have walked past your stand a couple of times and last time I was here, you very kindly answered all my questions. I see that the piece I am interested in is still here. But I have to tell you that I've also seen two or three similar pieces elsewhere at this fair. I'm a little embarrassed to say this, but although I like this one the best, it is a little more than I budgeted for. What is your very best price?'

That phrase, your very best price, is a term that dealers themselves frequently use and it means the lowest price at which a piece can be sold. Often, it never occurs to people that they can negotiate a price in this way.

On another occasion at Olympia an American and his wife walked up to my stand on the opening day with their interior decorator in tow. They unrolled the blueprints of the new mansion they were building in Beverly Hills and inspected my matching pair of Cantonese Chinese export Regency period (1830s) coffers. They were looking for two free-standing coffers decorated on all sides, which mine were, to use as tables next to a bed that was to be set in the middle of the room. They drove a very hard bargain, managing to get me down from the asking price of £7,000 to £6,000, all the while telling me about the $30 million they were lavishing on their nouveau palace. They wanted those two coffers and wouldn't leave until they had pared me down to the bone with a 'Take it or leave it buddy.' I was conscious of the rent of my stand and dinner to buy that evening, so I took it. I wish I could have said, 'I'm leaving it, buddy.'

People ask me if it is better to go to a fair on the first or the last day, I tell them, it all depends, which might not be a very helpful answer, but it really does depend. If you miss the first day you might miss some good things. Also on the first day a dealer is very much aware of his high overheads; perhaps he is worried that he won't break even. So, even on the first day he is looking to cover his costs. If you came to me on the last part of the fair whether we'd had a successful fair or not, like a lot of dealers at that stage we would probably be amenable to striking a bargain with you rather than taking the goods back home. I have often sold everything except for one or two pieces – a good fair – but I am still happy to negotiate.

My experience has shown me that more than half of the people who go to these fairs are there looking for a specific item, yet, suddenly they fall for something completely different – such as a lovely brass standard lamp when before they would never in their wildest dreams have thought of owning one. For these people, an antiques fair is like an Aladdin's cave – certainly it is more like a bazaar than the hushed environment of an antiques shop. And when this happens all of a sudden, they turn into enthusiastic bargain hunters.

I know I told you earlier to decide what you want and stick to it, but when you're feeling more confident, I think that, provided you are not too rash, it is actually not a bad thing to have an open mind if you are in a safe environment like a shop or a fair. (An auction, where auction fever can get hold of you, is another matter altogether – see page 54.)

Buying

at

Auction

When I first started out, dealers dominated auction sales, both as bidders and as sellers: often 95 per cent of any auction consisted of the trade with just five per cent of the public, who felt like outsiders, as indeed they were. I have to say it: dealers wanted to preserve the mystique, they wanted the public to buy their goods in their expensive shops. They didn't want the auction bartering to be seen in case (perish the thought!) customers in their shops started to haggle.

Television shows such as *The Antiques Roadshow*, and even my own television series, have changed all that. Since the 1980s auction sales of every type have become far more accessible to the public, to the extent that the proportion of dealers to ordinary people at auctions is now often reversed when collectables are being sold.

Even so, to many people, going to an auction is a terrifying prospect; many people still feel as if they are entering hallowed ground where the rituals and special language established by the high priest and the initiated (the auctioneer and the dealers) will baffle and confuse them. If you feel like this, the answer is to join them. Learn the language (it's all here in this book) and understand what they're on about. That way you will feel comfortable in that environment and you will no longer be an outsider.

Antiques auctions of all types are a rich source of goods, but always a minefield to the uninitiated. That doesn't mean that you can't take part and go to an auction or enjoy the thrill of bidding and eventually buying and taking home your desired object. You can, but don't be naïve. Learn to walk first of all before you run. And remember, there are guys like me around bidding against you, professionals who've had twenty, thirty years experience, so it's not as easy as all that.

These days auction houses are geared to help the first-time buyer and, despite what people say about scratching your nose and ending up with a Picasso, you are always in control: you and you alone decide whether to make that all-important bid or not. There is no doubt that auctions are conducted at such a rattling pace that panic can set in, and I must warn you that your first experience at an auction is nearly always nerve-racking. Not only is the first time you take a deep breath and raise your catalogue to catch the auctioneer's eye a bit like making your first speech in public, but the tension of listening to the other bids climb up and up, can give you clammy hands and make you feel sick. But if you have done your homework, know the ground rules and keep outwardly calm, all will go well.

What is an auction?

Essentially, there are five kinds of auction where you can buy antiques:

● **Quality auctions**, usually at the major auction houses where nothing but the best antiques – from furniture to paintings – are ever offered.

● **General sales**, where anything and everything from old to new – from that Greek urn to the kitchen sink – is up for sale.

● **Country house sales**, where the contents of that house are exclusively for sale in situ.

● **Private house and small business sales**, which are not as grand as country houses, and can include the contents of any kind of residence – from farms or seaside bungalows to family hotels that have gone broke.

● **Specialist and collectors' sales**, where you can go to bid for anything from garden and architectural pieces, stamps, carpets and rugs to ceramics or jewellery.

There are other kinds of auction sales where antiques hunting is possible, such as bankrupt stock sales, the ones conducted by the police consisting of unclaimed stolen goods, or unclaimed lost property sales held by the railway or bus companies, but in these places antiques will be thin on the ground so generally, you can disregard them if you are in search of a particular item. However, they are interesting to go to and there is always the very remote possibility that you might stumble across some unrecognized treasure. At least you'll have one advantage: it is most unlikely that there will be much competition from dealers in such sales.

Where to find them

Trade newspapers and magazines have completely changed the face of the antiques business. In the old days a local dealer might have been the kingpin of his district. He knew what was going on and, if anything special turned up in that area like the disposal of a house's contents, he would have it, or the cream of it, often sending the best items down to London to the big auction houses and making a handsome profit. Nowadays, with all trade newspapers and magazines advertising everything that's available, it's very much a free-for-all. Aware of what is coming up in the saleroom, people travel the country. Often now in a saleroom there'll be three or four phone calls, one from Hong Kong, two from America and one from France. The Internet has enabled many dealers to cast an even wider web.

It is worth pointing out here that many provincial auctioneers 'hold over' certain goods instead of putting them in a general sale. These are usually finer quality antiques, which they will 'save up' to lump together in one of the finer quality sales they hold perhaps two or three times a year to give their establishment some kudos and a bit of glamour.

For the seller the benefits are that these finer-quality sales are more widely advertised, and so more dealers will attend and the competition may be fiercer. The disadvantages are that your goods might sit around unsold for a considerable time, waiting for the sale. Sometimes, items that have been identified as being of particular interest and value might be whisked off to one of the provincial saleroom's big London branches. Again, this can be advantageous to the seller in that it will be properly identified and advertised.

For a buyer, there are pros and cons to this system. At a little local sale, where prices can be low, you can often get a good bargain; but prices can also be high if not much is for sale, when dealers might bid very strongly against each other out of pure boredom and a sense of competition. Equally, I have found that London prices can sometimes be surprisingly low because so much high-quality material is on offer. At the end of the day it really can be pot luck which way the market goes.

The first league salerooms are the big London ones. These also have smaller salerooms in major centres up and down the country. The big auction houses have many general antiques sales where an eclectic selection of quality goods is sold; they also pride themselves on their numerous specialist sales where one type of goods come up for sale perhaps once a year. The advantages of these specialist sales for a collector is that objects in your field are pulled together under one roof from all over the country, and perhaps even the world. Equally, the advantage for a seller is that there you will find the cream of collectors' items. The first-league salerooms are: Bonhams, Christie's, Sotheby's and Phillips.

A list of the second-league salerooms around the country, as well as the third and fourth league, and also a very useful list of specialist dealers, can be found in numerous trade publications such as *The Antique Gazette*.

I never seem to lose my passion for this business or get jaded. I go to a sale and the old adrenaline and excitement surges through me again. Sometimes I can barely control the excitement. Many times I have had to take a deep breath to calm myself down. In my head I can hear myself saying, 'I love it, I love it and I've got to have it!' This almost drooling enthusiasm isn't always good commercial sense, but I feel that if I can be enthusiastic about something, there must be something wonderful about it, and if I can infuse my clients with that passion, I will have given them something special too, a genuine love for the pieces they buy.

I've always been a little bit daring in that sense in business. I will go out and if I've got an allocation of money I will spend it all. Some people are a little more careful; they will keep some back for a rainy day. Before a sale has even begun they think, 'If I don't sell anything on again I'll be in a pickle', and I'm sure it infiltrates their attitude. I've always believed that you must get out there and pitch. Being on a knife-edge is part of the glamour and excitement of the game. Not everybody can take it – it can lead to depression and I've seen it crack people up – but I thrive on it. I also find that I don't make as many mistakes when it's costing me money. If I do make mistakes it's amazing how quickly I start to compensate for them and spend more time studying and inspecting because I know that not doing so enough can be costly for me.

The old dealers know all this, in fact, I'm just passing on to you what they passed on to me. 'You've got to back your own judgement,' they told me time and time again when I was

'If I **do** make **mistakes** it's amazing how quickly I start to **compensate** for them and spend more time studying and **inspecting** because I know that not doing so enough can be **costly** for me.'

starting out. There will be a time when you get a certain amount of confidence, and you will look at the points you've been told to look for, but there will also be a time when you're less confident and you've got to stand on your two feet for better or for worse. Don't be put off if you make a mistake; if you do, you've got to go back in there. There is no substitute for perseverance and you will build your confidence as you become more experienced.

And before I take you step by step through a typical auction (see page 52), let me give you the following very specific and helpful rules, which have stood me in good stead over the years.

Ten Golden Rules

1 Go to the preview

To decide what you want to buy, do your leg work. Find out about auctions where you can see the sorts of pieces you are interested in. Look in the trade press, appropriate glossy magazines or in local newspapers. Then go to the viewing. This will give you plenty of time to look, examine and ask questions. There is no sense in bidding for something that you have not thoroughly inspected. Even if you are a beginner, this inspection will tell you far more than you realized you knew. Have a cup of coffee, go back and have another look. Then sleep on it.

2 Get a condition report

This is invaluable if you are a beginner. You can ask the auctioneer to give you one (see page 55). For a substantial piece, you can ask a dealer you know and pay him.

3 On the day of the sale, get there in good time and register

Many people arrive late and miss the boat. Even if the item you are bidding for is to be auctioned late in the sale, you will still gain a lot from familiarizing yourself with the saleroom environment and watching the prices. You must register because when you do you will be given a paddle or a card with a number on it to hold up so that the auctioneer can keep track of who is bidding for what.

4 Know what you want and bid only for the pieces that you have inspected

This sounds like unnecessary advice, but you'd be surprised how many people change their mind at the last moment and start to bid for something they haven't inspected. Or, if they have lost the piece they were after, they are determined to go home with something for their pains but frequently end up with any old rubbish.

Even when I know what I want at an auction, I will often inspect several other likely pieces that I am undecided about. If the bidding for any of those pieces is sluggish I will sometimes bid for it, but not unless I have thoroughly inspected it first. I did have a disaster once which taught me a lesson I've never forgotten (see page 66). If you don't inspect the piece before bidding, don't be surprised if you end up with rubbish. It is far better to walk away than buy a turkey – there will always be other sales and other antiques to buy.

5 Have a budget and stick to it

Again, in the frenzy of the moment you might be determined to buy something at any cost. The trouble is that it might cost you dear, far more than you can afford or the piece is worth. Sometimes people are very circumspect and buy their piece within their budget, but then, fired with success, they go auction crazy and bid for the next six lots. Don't.

6 Don't lose what you want for a bid

This is the converse of rule five, but there are times when rule five doesn't apply – when acquiring an item means more than the price. If a piece is special to you, go for it. That one last bid might win the day. But don't go crazy. Use your instinct, judge when to continue that last half-inch and when to stop. Even having said that, I would say that sometimes, if you really fall in love with something, you should buy it no matter what the cost. It might end up costing more than you can afford, but the price won't be unrealistic in the market-place because it is a truism that the market value will be just one bid more than the next bidder. At times like that you have to let your heart rule your head or else you will always regret it.

7 Go for quality

I've said it before and I'll say it again. Quality counts. It is the reason you are buying antiques.

8 Let the auctioneer know that you are bidding

It used to be said that people wore false moustaches at auctions and twitched an eyebrow to indicate a bid, but unless you are bidding for a Renoir worth millions and feel the need to fool the opposition, such games are unnecessary. Let the auctioneer see that you are bidding by raising your catalogue or paddle; if you don't he might miss your obscure signal. And when you have finished bidding, tell him 'No' with a firm shake of your head.

9 Don't get auction fever

I've seen this so many times. It's like a feeding frenzy at the zoo or the Klondike gold rush. The most rational people can suddenly bid for everything at any price. Reality only hits home when they see how much they have spent and realize they have to arrange the transport home of half the contents of the auction room. Don't do it.

10 Remember the hidden costs

The buyer's commission or premium varies from one saleroom to another. Generally it's 15 per cent. It should be in the catalogue. If it's not, find out what it is when you register and mentally add it on to your bid. VAT is standard – currently $17\frac{1}{2}$ per cent on the commission only, not on the full bid price.

Transport can also prove expensive. Take it all into account – it can add up to an extra £18 on every £100 under the hammer.

You also need to check removal time. Normally, if you leave your goods hanging around the auction room for more than 24 hours you will be charged storage.

Taking the plunge

If you feel intimidated by auctions, first attend an auction without even thinking of buying. Inspect at the preview, watch the sale go through, watch the prices. Get the feel of it. When you feel ready, if you hear of a sale and see something in the catalogue you like, and the estimates are within a price range to suit your pocket, it would be fine to dip your toes into the water and plan on making that first crucial bid.

I use the word 'plan' because that is exactly what you should do. Say you want to buy a table, as I once did many years ago when I was furnishing my first home. The first thing to do is go to the preview and inspect that table thoroughly. Put your hands on it and feel the wood. Is that a century of hand waxing, or is that modern varnish? Get a sense of the weight; solid mahogany and oak are heavy. What about the way the table stands – does it wobble, and are the legs uneven or loose? Look underneath, a place that restorers and fakers often neglect: is it held together with new brackets or odd blocks of wood, or is there fresh stain? Good common sense will tell you if you can say to yourself, 'Well that looks pretty good value for money to me. They're saying £400–£600 – and remember, add 18 per cent. I can afford that. It seems like a very nice piece of furniture for that price range.'

At this stage there are a number of things you need to know about auction sales – and the way they work and the options available to you.

Condition report

You're not an antiques expert, but you've got plenty of grey matter up there, and it's a matter of just applying it. If you lack experience and knowledge and you are thinking of bidding for a very expensive piece, there is a very easy way of safeguarding yourself: call a representative of the saleroom, either the saleroom manager or, with the bigger salerooms, the head of department, and ask for a condition report. This is perfectly normal and they won't throw up their hands in horror at being asked. A condition report is a written or verbal statement about the piece you are interested in. In simple language it will say what it is, describe it, give the date or approximate date of manufacture, tell you any faults and give a value based on the expert's experience and the market-place.

Representation

You might consider visiting a local antiques dealer to represent you in the saleroom. If you do agree a fee or a commission, he will go to the preview and advise you on what to bid for. In this way you can utilize his experience in exactly the same way as you would get the AA to vet a car you want to buy, or a surveyor to inspect a house before you take out a mortgage. People are used

'In **my opinion** there is nothing so satisfying as a hands-on **approach** when you're dealing with **antiques.**'

to doing such things as a matter of course, yet it never occurs to them to do the same for a table and a set of chairs that might cost £2,000 or £3,000.

For those with little time, a good dealer can save a client a lot of time and trouble. Of course everyone is in the business to make money – it would be foolish to deny it – but because of his greater expertise a dealer can actually save you money.

You can also ask someone from the auction house to represent you at the sale. On the day of the sale you will probably notice that not all bids are from the floor. In a grand sale, especially if an important picture or *objet d'art* is being auctioned, you might notice a battery of saleroom assistants lined up on telephones. They will be taking telephone bids from absentee buyers or clients who are on the other end of the telephone – perhaps people from overseas who could not attend in person, people who do not wish their identity to be known by their rivals. Another way of making an absentee bid, one known as a commission bid, is to pre-arrange your bid with the auctioneer. Suppose, for example, that a piece has been estimated at £4,000–£5,000. You might be prepared to go up to £8,000. The final bid from the floor or the telephone is £7,500. The auctioneer will then bring your bid into play and you win the day. Of course, if someone else comes in at £8,500 you are gazumped and they win.

But these kind of deals are for the high-flyers. My advice to you would be to always attend in person or you will never get the feel of this business; and even with all my experience I personally would be very reluctant to be an absentee bidder. In my opinion there is nothing so satisfying as a hands-on approach when you're dealing with antiques.

The reserve price

This is the lowest price that the seller will accept. The auctioneer sets it, using his experience in conjunction with the seller. Some auctioneers are renowned for valuing low, the advantage being that it attracts a lot more people, especially in the trade.

If I see that a local auctioneer has put a pair of 19th-century library globes at £4,000–£6.000, and I know on a bad day they're worth £12,000, I will go rushing along to the auction, along with all the other dealers. Ten to one, at the end of the day the globes will make £16,000, perhaps because a little competition gets going in that room full of dealers. But this approach can be very misleading to a private person, who is led to believe that the guide of £4,000–£6,000 is where they should be pitching their bids.

Some sellers will argue with the auctioneer. They think that if they put down a very high reserve it will automatically lead to the auctioneer setting a higher estimate. The auctioneer might say, 'Madam, this ashtray you've brought along is very nice and I think it should fetch £400–£600.' Mrs Smythe-Jones replies, 'Well, I was hoping to get a bit more than that, Mr Robinson,' to which the auctioneer might say, 'Well, we could try £600–£800, with a reserve of £600 if you give me a little flexibility.' But normally, the auctioneer will advise the seller to keep it to the lower estimate because the auction house gets commission only if it sells the goods. Auctioneers also like to surprise the client by saying, 'By the way, that ashtray that we said £400–£600, there was a great demand for it and it made £1,200.' To which, if the script is written as he hopes, Mrs Smythe-Jones will reply, 'I'm very pleased, Mr Robinson. I'll bring along some more of my very nice things for you to sell in your saleroom.'

The sale price

If I go into a saleroom and I see a table estimated at £400–£600 my experience of hundreds of similar tables tells me whether that's a reasonable estimate or not. Sometimes I may look at that table and recognize that there is something special about it, and it's often an intangible thing. I will say to myself, 'What a beauty! That's the nicest example I have ever seen.'

When the bidding passes £600 and gets up to £1,500, then £2,200 then £2,800 I don't blink, and keep going. My experience has kicked in and is telling me to keep bidding because I know that's the best example I've seen in twenty-odd years. I may never see another one with that same quality, so I'll give a strong price to buy it. This is where the pocket and the heart come in.

If you are a private individual who has been guided by the £400–£600 price range, you're comfortable within that framework, but once the bidding starts spiralling way beyond that you become confused. You think, 'What's going on?' This is why the professional has a great advantage: his experience and knowledge kicks in to tell him to keep bidding long after the novice has dropped out. This is not always the case. Sometimes a private buyer with a lot of money gets caught up in the chase and senses the excitement. He says to himself, 'I want that. If they can bid, so can I. If it's worth £2,200 to a dealer, who must sell at a profit, it's worth that to me.' Entrepreneurial instincts take over and the private buyer sticks in there. The auction environment can be a very exciting and stimulating one and many people who would never dream of throwing their money away in a casino get into auction frenzy. Believe me, I've seen it happen. I have even seen husband and wife bid against each other unaware that the other is bidding. I am painting an exceptional scenario here, but it is one that you might encounter. I do not recommend that you join the chase. Remember rule five: have a budget and stick to it.

Competition

For no apparent reason, some sales attract an awful lot of attention from dealers and they swarm in from all over the country like bees to a honey pot. Sometimes 20 to 30 dealers gathering at an auction is fine if there are plenty of quality goods available to be shared out. But if quality is thin on the ground they start to battle it out for the most ordinary pieces and prices can spiral out of all proportion to the value. For the innocent amateur this can be quite baffling. Just bear in mind that sometimes these things do happen and, if you are a beginner at your very first auction, stick to my rules and don't let such a situation put you off.

Let me give you an example of a common sequence of events. I go to what seems to be a very inexpensive saleroom in the middle of a cattleyard somewhere, drawn there by information from my runner who has spotted a 'sleeper'. It's a late Regency cabinet that has been lying in an attic for a century and is so encrusted with dirt that you don't know what it is; but the original pristine piece is underneath in all its glory, just waiting to be rediscovered. But other runners who work for other dealers have also spotted that cabinet. On my arrival to preview I think, 'That little beauty is coming home with me – these guys here with straw in their hair certainly won't be recognizing this.' But as I wait around for the sale to start, other dealers start popping up from behind chiffoniers and I realize there's going to be a terrible massacre.

'We've **all** had our moments of **madness** though, so don't feel **too upset** if you get a touch of auction **fever** from time to time.'

If you've got up at the crack of dawn, driven for three hours, viewed the material, stayed another three hours until the sale commences and then have another three hours' drive home after your lot has been dispensed with, it can make for a lot more determination. The same thing applies to your competitors. 'Aw my Gawd, there's so and so! I've come all this way down here to buy this cabinet and I'm not going to leave without it.'

Sometimes, good sense and all the lessons I've been teaching you kick in and I walk away. We've all had our moments of madness though, so don't feel too upset if you get a touch of auction fever from time to time.

Runners

Someone you might see at an auction sale is a runner. Runners were a good system in the past when there were no trade newspapers or magazines. You still find them today: people who make a living by going round all sorts of outlets for antiques, spotting goods and calling the appropriate dealers. They live by getting commission, the amount of which varies, depending on how much the dealer makes; it may not be a percentage on the value of the item, but could still be a few hundred pounds, especially if they have directed the dealer to a very good or interesting piece.

How much is it worth?

If you're thinking of selling something at auction, you'll want to know, before you decide, what the piece is likely to fetch. You can buy books filled with photographs of items of every category of antiques, decorative items and memorabilia from salerooms the length and breadth of the British Isles, together with the price they fetched on the day of sale. I'm not sure what this information tells you, because something can bring a very good price and if that price is then inserted in the book you presume that that is the going price for an 18th-century walnut bureau bookcase, or whatever, but it may not be the case. The one in the book could be a real corker that is worth, say, £36,000. You think, 'Ah, that's the price.' But it's not true for a very poor one in terrible condition that goes for £4,000–£5,000. Or the one in the book wasn't a corker – it just made a high price because it was a good day.

Using price guides can work against you. Say you have a prized 18th-century walnut bureau bookcase at home that you inherited from your great-aunt. You look in one of these price-guide books, and your eyes light up. You hadn't intended to sell, but now, with a potential £36,000 staring you in the face, you decide that you will, so that you can buy that cottage in France or pay for your daughter's school fees. Then, when the auctioneer advises you it will not get much above £6,000 and at the auction it reaches only £4,000, who do you blame, the auctioneer or the book? Certainly you might feel you're being cheated in some way, but in fact it is virtually impossible to say how much something is worth just by comparing it with a photograph in a book of something you don't know the condition of.

If I were to take three identical bookcases such as the lovely little French one that I have in my sitting room at home and place them in three different auctions in this country, they would bring three totally different prices that would not only be based on their present condition, but would also depend on the competition at the saleroom on that particular day.

You can learn a lot from price-guide books about size, shape, materials and style. Use them as a rough guide to price by all means, but don't depend on them. Using them is not as good as getting out there yourself, asking questions, seeking advice and learning by your own experience.

Buyer beware

In a saleroom there is very much a 'buyer beware' situation which you aren't warned about in a very obvious way, so it's up to you to familiarize yourself with all the 'catches'. At the back of the catalogue you will find a huge list of disclaimers

'Certainly you **might** feel you're being **cheated** in some way, but in fact it is virtually **impossible** to say how much something is **worth** just by comparing it with a **photograph** in a book of something you **don't** know the condition of.'

about the sale in fairly small print, which you should read and make sure you know about.

Auction houses

Auction houses, country house sales and specialist sales are essentially the same thing: they are places where goods are sold under the hammer to a bidder. But there are differences in standard between them all.

Quality auction houses

At the top of the tree are the four grand ones – Phillips, Sotheby's, Bonhams and Christie's (all of which have a number of branches around the country) where you will get good-quality pieces. But the fact that these are grand establishments with often millions of pounds' worth of high-class goods for sale doesn't mean that you can't go and have a look. In fact, it's an excellent idea to wander in off Bond Street or St James's next time you are in London on a viewing day – it will be excellent practice in developing a 'good eye' for antiques because what you will see is likely to be of the best quality and will give you a yardstick when assessing pieces elsewhere. You won't always find furniture on display. Often, specialist sales are held, of anything from statues and busts to stamps or carpets, and at other times the entire 'contents' of someone's home is up for sale, and in this case there will usually be a mix of antiques and new items, as there was at the recent sale of the house contents of Elton John's manager, John Read, where there was a wonderful mix of good, original antiques, decorator-inspired pieces, modern dinner services and stylish gifts he had been given over the years, such as Lalique glass and bejewelled Swiss watches. Or perhaps the sale will consist of pop memorabilia or couturier clothing – the sale of the late Princess of Wales' designer frocks came under this type of sale (although the sale was in New York there was a viewing in London). Whatever is on sale, you will enjoy the experience and will almost certainly learn something. Again, don't be intimidated.

MICHAEL 'DICK' TURPIN

In the days when I was a newcomer to the business, buying modest things at sales, there was always something in my price range that I could take away. But major dealers bought the very best – Chippendale furniture, grand tapestries that I could only gawp at. These men were like the movie stars of the day – you ogled them and listened to them and paid court to them as they told their tales.

One of these was Michael Turpin. Michael, otherwise known as Dick, has a shop in central London. He has been in this business almost for ever – 40 or 50 years? It be might even more. He is recognized as one of the greatest authorities on English 18th-century furniture in the world. He is a huge imposing man with a walrus moustache and a booming voice you can hear from every corner of a saleroom, bawling out, 'That is no effing good!' Known to use more than a few swear words, he is, I think, the most charismatic larger-than-life character I have ever met. He is still in business, highly respected because he has seen it all and done it all.

I was at Christie's recently, viewing a major sale of walnut furniture and happened to bump into Dick Turpin, walking around with his lady (who, incidentally, used to work as my assistant in my shop in Manchester). On display were something like 20 or 30 walnut bachelor chests, as rare as hens' teeth today. Dick strolled past them all, firing off comments: 'No effing good, no effing good, no effing good, that's all right, no effing good, I remember that one in the forties: it was no effing good then and it's no effing good now!' He'd seen them all. He even knew who had repaired them in the 1920s and 1930s – good restorers who made small adjustments, experienced in working with walnut. He is typical of a type of old-fashioned dealer; if ever you want to know anything, ask Dick, because he will share his knowledge with you.

Once at a major London sale of important English furniture, where a fairly youngish auctioneer was taking his run at the rostrum, a pair of console tables came up. 'Ladies and gentlemen, Lot No 56 – a pair of 18th-century console tables.' From the back of the room came a loud bellow: 'They're no effing good and they never were any effing good!'

The place went silent. Anybody else would have been escorted from the room unceremoniously, but the auctioneer looked up and realized it was the Governor. Obviously the sale proceeded, but notice was taken of Dick's opinion. If Dick Turpin said it was so, it was so.

On another occasion I went on to his stand at an international show in London and, showing interest, not to purchase but to admire, I commented, 'What a wonderful pair of chairs.' To which I heard the deep rumble, 'They effing ought to be. They're by the man himself – Mr Chippendale!'

INSPECT, INSPECT, INSPECT!

Many years ago when I was new to the business I went to a country sale in Carmarthen. It took me a day to get there, and when I arrived I viewed everything I was interested in thoroughly, inside out and upside down. I stayed the night and was at the saleroom early the next day. Waiting for my particular lot to come along, suddenly I heard the auctioneer say. 'Ladies and gentlemen, who'll start me at £1,000 for this wonderful Victorian seven-piece salon suite?'

There was a deathly hush as he scanned the room. 'OK, who'll start me at £500? I'll start on a little less. Who'll start at £200? Are there no takers? No one going to bid for this wonderful suite? Ladies and gentlemen, this is absolutely for nothing! Are you sure you're not going to bid? Who will give me £200?'

The bargain hunter in me suddenly woke up. 'Oh blimey, there's something cheap going here!' Up went my hand. *Bang* went the hammer. 'SOLD!'

It was only when I inspected the suite that I found it was riddled with woodworm. Four pieces were as spongy as Aero bars, and if you touched them they fell apart. Of the seven pieces I took three away, leaving four heaps of junk in the saleroom. From then on I never, ever, bought a piece of furniture or an object, no matter how flowery the description from the rostrum or how cheap it was. Learn from me – always inspect!

General salerooms

These places are very much the poor cousins of the grander antiques houses, but they bring back great memories for me. When I set out 25 years ago as a dealer, I started off with general sales. They're a good place to cut your teeth and get a feel of the business if you're not looking for anything of a very high quality. But if you hunt around, there are still bargains and interesting things to be found, often as cheap as chips. For a first-time buyer I would recommend going to a local auction in a saleroom in some little market town. It will be small, but your head won't reel from looking at too much, too soon. You will find plenty to interest you, but not so much that you can't take it all in in a couple of hours. If you are at this stage, don't even think about buying until you feel confident. Observe, learn and familiarize yourself with what might seem a frightening environment. It won't be long before you feel perfectly at ease.

Many decorators come to general sales looking for things they can tart up. For example, at a recent sale I spotted a pair of late Georgian bedposts so grey that they had obviously been out in the rain or in a leaky barn for decades. They were down for an estimated £60–£80. But someone with a keen eye knew that with a little oil and wax to restore the colour, they would be worth something. In the event, they went for £280, and I knew that the next time I saw them they would be in *Homes and Gardens* with chintz all around them.

But if you are a serious buyer I would hesitate to send you to a sale of this nature, even if you had very modest means, since it is rare to find anything of quality. I would rather send you to a country auction or a country house sale. Even at a grand country house there are nice pieces for reasonable prices to be found. There are a lot of trade rejects thrown into a general saleroom. Here, you will find an absolute mish-mash of goods, usually in quite a poor condition. In big cities you will often find goods that antiques dealers have been unable to sell or rejects from bigger sales. You will find the contents of modest homes up for grabs. Now and then, you might spot something special that has slipped though the net. But I should add that the last time I was at Christie's general goods saleroom in South Kensington, I spotted a runner – and if he was there, you can bet that others, too, were likely to be there during the course of the preview. Nothing much of any worth would escape their eagle eyes for a hopeful novice to snap up.

I have seen some remarkable things in salerooms where pieces have been underestimated by the auctioneer. At one country sale, an old woman put her treasured walnut Queen Anne bureau bookcase up for sale. She had just sold her little terraced cottage for about £10,000 and was convinced that a piece of furniture must be worth proportionately less. As the bidding started and bids for the bookcase rose, someone had to get her a hardback chair and a glass of water because she nearly fainted. When it went for £14,000 under the hammer I think she did swoon. All the other chattels in the house were ordinary cottagey bits and pieces, but her parents had worked in a grand country house and had been given the Queen Anne piece after 40 years' service. Today, of course, the value of such a bookcase could be over £50,000, but it's all relative – how many terraced cottages can you still buy for £10,000?

Country house sales

There was a time in the fifties and sixties when grand country houses and stately homes were being emptied and pulled down by the dozens every year and their contents sold for a song. That was the time to buy, and I suspect that many people did, often buying massive pieces that would have looked wonderful in rooms 18.5m (60ft) long and 4.5m (15ft) high, but were impossible to fit in their more modest homes. As a result, sadly, many pieces were hacked down and cut to fit. Magnificent Georgian bureau-bookcases lost their top halves; bookcases and wardrobes lost their ornate pediments; tall boys became lowboys, and leaves of fine mahogany tables were discarded and chopped up to make bookshelves or even – horrors – firewood!

Country house sales might have passed their manic heyday, but there are still plenty of them to be found, giving us all a chance to poke around in another world and perhaps dream a little. They are a glamorous environment and can provide a wonderful day out with an added opportunity to buy a small slice of history. Country house sales come in all styles and sizes, from the very grand, such as Luton Hoo, Bedfordshire, which was recently on the market, lock, stock and barrel, or Eaton Hall, the Duke of Westminster's former stately pile when the Duke, the richest landowner in England, built a smaller, more modern house in the grounds of the old one. Whatever the reason for the sale of the contents, you will often

RUPERT SPENCER

AN OLD FASHIONED AUCTIONEER

In the Yorkshire area a local firm, Henry Spencer, used to hold some wonderful country house sales as grand house after house tumbled to taxes and
deaths, marking the end of dynasties. The auctioneer was Rupert Spencer,
an elderly man when I started in the business, a real old-fashioned auctioneer and great charmer. He'd get up on to the rostrum at about five to ten on
the nail, and welcome everybody. 'Ladies and gentlemen, we are about to
start this dispersal sale of the so-and-so family at such-and-such hall which
has been the family's home for 300 years. I would like to welcome here this
morning Mr John Phillips from Bond Street, Mr Arnold Singer from
Mayfair, Mr So-and-So from Mallets over there' – all illustrious dealers of
some standing. He would go through the list, and then he'd start on the
local regular private buyers: 'Mr and Mrs Silver, how nice to see you again –
I hope you take away something wonderful from the sale today.' He would
go on to say, 'I've checked with Reuters this morning and there is only one
Hindu altar being sold in this country today.' Finally, he would say, quoting
Keats: 'Ladies and gentlemen, spend your money wisely, buy the best
objects you can, and always remember a thing of beauty is a joy for ever! It's
ten o'clock and let's start the sale with Lot No. 1!'

see merchandise collected over many hundreds of years, over
many generations. The ambience is very special and it sometimes drives people into giving £200 or £300 for a 1930s
electric fire! We call that particular madness 'country house
fever' and I have to admit that even dealers have been known
to succumb to it, so beguiling is the sense of history and
romance of the setting, particularly on a lazy summer's day
when the scent of roses and hay meadows drifts in through
open windows and the rooms smell of centuries of beeswax.

One of the earliest country house sales I attended was in
Yorkshire at a marvellous place, Old Brabham Hall, where there
was a wide selection of things, from the grand down to the very
ordinary. At the viewing, I spotted a pair of decanters of exquisite

quality, etched with the Prince of Wales' feathers. The estimate of £200–£300 was within my price range and I thought they were special, so I started to go into the bidding. Suddenly it was up to £500, then £600. Long after I had dropped out, canny dealers kept going and going, ever upwards; finally, the decanters went for £3,000, a huge sum over 20 years ago. Older dealers with more experience knew what I wasn't aware of: these decanters were by a specific glassmaker and had belonged to the Prince of Wales, who had given them to a member of the family. I was told there were known to be just four pairs in existence, the Queen having the other three pairs.

Sadly we will never see the likes of some of the sales I've been to again. I honestly think I witnessed the passing of an era. I recall going to a sale on the Scottish borders of Lord Dalhousie's possessions. He had been the viceroy of India in the later part of the 19th century and had amassed a treasure trove of collectables – the mind-blowing collection of things that were there will never be gathered again under one roof. There were even copies of Tipu's throne carved in wood in Indian workshops and gilded – the original was in gold – and Tipu's infamous beheading sword.

Some of the grand places where sales were held were the homes of military families going back some 200 or 300 years. From tours of duty all over the world, to India, China, Africa, members of the family had brought back furniture and objects the likes of which you'll never see again. I remember once seeing a framed flag in one of those country houses that was the very one removed from the Summer Palace in Peking during the Boxer Rebellion.

Going to a country house sale

Country house sales are advertised well in advance in many of the more upmarket Sunday newspapers, glossy magazines such as *Country Life* or *Homes and Gardens* as well as in the trade press. It is always advisable to send off for a catalogue, because not only will it give you a detailed inventory of what is for sale, but it will also give you an estimated price guide, and it will save you from wasting your time if you are looking for a particular object like a garden statue or an oak settle.

Sometimes, you might be on holiday or on a drive in the country when you see signs or posters directing you to a sale. Many people decide on impulse to a visit to such a sale and go with no intention of buying – they just want a nice drive with an interesting destination and a good look at how the wealthy live. But beware, you need a strong will not to bid for something or another in the heat of the moment.

Whether you are buying or not, my advice to you would be to get to the sale the day before, if it is local; or even consider staying overnight in the village pub or some nice bed and

'From tours of duty **all** over the **world**, to India, China, Africa, members of the family had brought back **furniture** and **objects** the likes of which you'll **never** see again.'

breakfast so that you can make a thorough inspection of the goods at a leisurely pace. On the day of the sale, even if you get there the moment the gates are opened, there will almost certainly be so many other people crammed in that you will find it almost impossible to inspect the goods.

Take a floor plan of your house and the dimensions of all your rooms and of furniture already in those rooms that you want to keep. Something in a grand house with panelled walls and acres of polished floorboards can look charming and quite petite, but once you've got it home it can be a real white elephant, and as big as one.

Have some idea of what you want, and never, ever, buy on the spur of the moment unless the lot you can't resist is going for just for a pound or two, because the chances are that you won't know what to do with three torn leather poufs and a stuffed squirrel under a cracked bell jar.

Remember, if you intend to bid, that you must register, so that the auctioneer will know you are a serious buyer. Usually, registering will include giving your name, address and telephone number and proposed method of payment should your bid be lucky. You should also enquire how much the buyer's premium or 'commission' is. As with auctions, you must also arrange for the removal of your goods within a certain period of time (usually 24 hours); otherwise you will be charged storage. The auctioneer can help you with this if necessary.

Values and prices change according to the mood and market. Recently, I was at the preview of the house contents of a famous and very wealthy person and was surprised at how modest the estimated prices were for most of the more decorative items. You could have bought top-quality glass, silver and leather goods and some nicely framed prints for less than £100. This reflected the slightly cautious mood in the market and also, changes in fashion. Many of the items were quite flamboyant at a time when interior designers have decreed that the minimalist look is in. Two years before these items would have been fiercely contested and the estimates would have taken that into account.

If you are a serious buyer but everything inside the house is way beyond your means, get out into the outbuildings. Have a thorough scour around, because sometimes in these great houses a lot of nice but broken things were discarded to the stables or old wash-houses and a little judicious repair could be all that something needs.

If you find something like this, inspect the piece carefully and use your common sense to judge whether it is broken beyond repair. Is it so spongy and riddled with woodworm that you can push your finger into the wood? If it's a chair, is the back broken, or if it's a table, does it have only three legs? Has the walnut veneer lifted or bubbled where someone has watered a pot plant? If it's a cupboard, are the hinges broken, are the jambs split? Does a Georgian card table gape and 'smile' at you? Is a Sèvres porcelain vase badly cracked; has that Wedgwood teapot lost its spout and lid? You have to ask yourself 'when does an original turn into a liquorice allsort (a piece that is a mixture of two or more items)? If there are any obvious, major faults, walk away. The cost of restoration will be far too much.

Once I went to a sale in Parr in Cornwall, at the type of house where you went down a driveway that went for about 5.5km (3½ miles) through a park full of deer grazing under mature trees hundreds of years old. In the house each room had a mixture of furniture from Georgian right back to Elizabethan and about 1500 when the family was first established, and displayed wonderfully exotic things they had brought back from all over the world as they flourished and ruled all the pink patches on the old atlases. On the staircase from top to bottom were portraits of ancestors, finishing at the bottom with an 18-year-old first lieutenant who had died at the Battle of the Somme, the last of the male line. It was his sister who had passed away; and the contents were being sold by Cornwall County Council, who had inherited everything, all that history, in the old lady's will, and were turning the house into an old people's home.

I walked into the dining room and there was an oil painting that must have been 4.5m (14ft) long, depicting the Battle of the Nile in the 18th century, in the forefront of which was one of the ancestors I'd seen on the staircase wall, the Admiral Saul Gravesaul, who was number two to Nelson at the battle. There were items in the family collection, such as a bosun's whistle, given as a present by Nelson to the Admiral and trophies taken round the world. These wonderful exciting contents were to be dispersed and would be gone for ever. I was there at the dismantling of something like 400 years of military and naval history, the sale of trophies taken from battles and naval engagements and relics of one extinct family's time in high office.

In those days there were such exciting things to buy. You could wander into an outbuilding and who knew what you might find in the bottom of a croquet box?

Private house sales

I have been to many sales in quite modest homes, where, perhaps following the death of a well-loved parent, the heirs decide to sell everything and split the proceeds. Sometimes farmers die and their possessions are sold because they have no heir to follow them; or, in these hard times, farmers might go bankrupt and there's a sale where everything is up for grabs, including the cows, the pigs, the milk churns and the tractors. In such cases, you might be lucky and discover that the house or farm, however humble, has been in the family for generations, and that there are some charming, original antiques just waiting to be discovered. Hotels, especially country-house hotels, for which there was a fad in the eighties, are other places where total contents are often sold.

Such sales are usually advertised in local newspapers. It is only worth spending money for national advertising for the grander country house sales. Many farm sales are advertised on posters nailed to trees around the farm, so if you are out for a drive, you could keep a sharp eye out. I would advise against just 'dropping in' on the actual day of the sale because you will never have time to inspect the goods and ten to one you will be caught up in auction fever. However, if a small sale is advertised in your area it is well worth going along the day before to inspect the goods because you will find that usually only local people will attend the sale and you won't be competing against high flyers and dealers from all over the country. But bear in mind that anything of local or county interest, such as a painting of a local view or a piece of memorabilia relating to a well-known character from those parts, will excite a lot of local interest and will fetch quite a high price.

Recently, I attended a sale in a handsome little farmhouse with a couple who were looking for a large painting or some

'In those days there were such exciting things to buy. You could wander into an outbuilding and who knew what you might find in the bottom of a croquet box?'

BUDGETING

THE FOLLOWING STORY of a trip to a specialist sale is a good example of when it's best to apply the rule of having a budget and sticking to it.

Jane, who was landscaping her garden, was looking for an architectural piece to make a statement and as a focal point in a patio area, where she intended holding small garden parties and wine tastings in her business as a wine seller. She decided that, out of her quite substantial overall budget for her landscaping, she could spend £600–£800 on a feature piece, which seemed reasonable for a statue or a large urn.

By looking through the trade press, I discovered a specialist sale of garden furniture and related architectural pieces in Edinburgh. It was a long way to go, but as I have said before, antiques hunting can be fun. You can have a nice outing or a mini-break and see a bit of the country. I sent off for the catalogue and we looked through it before we left. Many of the pieces were more expensive than Jane could afford, but there were one or two nice ones with a wine theme, so she decided to attend the sale despite the distance.

It's a good thing we went in person and didn't put in a phone bid because one of the pieces that had attracted her eye, a grape press, turned out to be far smaller than it looked in the catalogue. In fact, I was sure that it wasn't a grape press at all, but the bottom half of something or other. Several stunning garden seats were rejected because the estimates were far too high. Then Jane came across a

prints to fill a space on the sitting-room wall of their Victorian house. I found the sale advertised in the trade press within an easy drive, allowing us time to go the day before to inspect, and I'm glad that we did, because on the actual day of the sale the place was packed. It was a small local sale, so few dealers came, which can always help to keep prices down. The couple were quite taken with some regional maps and scenes and I advised them that in this case local interest would push the prices very high, as it did. Instead they ended up by buying some delightful signed lithographs by John Leitch, the cartoonist who worked for Punch, which were totally in keeping with their room and with the other engravings already on the walls, and were well within the estimated pair of elegant, wrought-iron gates. She had not previously considered these as a feature when we went through the catalogue, but in the flesh, they were stylish and within her budget. 'They're perfect!' she enthused. 'I'll go for them.'

I told her that if she got them, she should leave them exactly as they were, encrustations and all, and certainly she should not attempt to 'restore' them with a lick of shiny whiter-than-white paint. And then I murmured a word of caution: 'They are Regency or early Victorian. There will be a lot of people and dealers bidding for them, so if the price starts to escalate, *stick to your budget, but don't lose them for a bid.*'

It turned out that this was good advice. The gates went for £1,700 to another bidder – well over £2,300 with the commission, VAT and transport. Now, someone of less steely backbone might have been so keen to buy something after going all that way that he would have cast caution to the winds and bid wildly, ending up with something that broke his budget. It's true that sometimes hesitation can bring disappointment, but spending more than you intended can be depressing.

Yes, it was disappointing to return home empty-handed. But, as Jane told me, she had enjoyed the experience of an auction, she had learned a great deal, and she was determined to keep looking.

And that, in a nutshell is what antiques hunting is all about: the thrill of the chase, the enjoyment of the day, looking, learning, not losing your head and wanting to continue through the many disappointments along the way, and what you will end up with are some lovely pieces in your home that will give you years of pleasure.

price. I have no doubt that had these particular cartoons been in a major specialist sale in one of the big auction houses they would have gone for a lot more. I tell this story because it's important to know if there is any local connection with some piece you are anxious to buy and set your bid accordingly.

Specialist collectors' auctions

Specialist sales for collectors now make up 50 per cent of all auctions. If you're trying to build up a collection of certain items, you will quickly become an expert at knowing where to look and, by getting a specialist magazine or newsletter from other collectors, you will hear of any upcoming sales. For example, there are big Beatles fairs and conventions several times a year, not just in this country but also in Europe and the United States, where collectors sell and trade. But it will quickly be obvious that at any place where ardent collectors go there will be strong competition and prices will reflect this.

Recently I went with Olga and Olga, a mother and daughter, to buy an Oriental rug. What we call Oriental carpets covers Turkish, Afghan, Armenian, Chinese and of course, Persian carpets. Usually they have a pile, even if it is a shaved one. Not all valuable carpets are Oriental: the Europeans created their own, flatter-woven carpets which are more like tapestry, such as Aubusson ones from France, which are renowned for their flower designs and soft, pastel colours.

Carpets are not a specialist area of mine, but by talking to rug and carpet dealers with a lifetime of experience I was able to glean the state of the market; and the in-house expert was on hand to offer advice. I said to him, 'This is not really my field. Am I right in thinking that the best example in terms of wear, tear, colour and quality, will bring the best price, and is that the best way to go?' He replied, 'Yes, David. Exactly the same rule applies as in furniture. Look for the best example.'

Carpets get worn, and you should look for the one in the best condition. Colour is important, as is design. If you can't afford the one you've decided is the best, buy the best you can within your budget. If it's the case that the best you can afford is slightly smaller than the size you wanted, then buy a slightly smaller one. Cut your cloth down to size. Just because you want something big, don't buy something second rate.

While all auction sales are conducted in exactly the same way – the viewing, the registration, the bid – there are little flourishes that belong to certain specialist areas. With a carpet sale you will walk in and find that it looks like a Turkish bazaar, with hundreds of carpets of every size hanging from the walls and the bigger ones piled up in sofa-high heaps in the centre of the floor. Now you would be quite right in asking, 'How on earth can I see the carpets at the bottom of the pile?' Don't worry – four times a day there is an event called the turning of the carpets, when saleroom porters line up (very much like the centre court tarpaulin pullers at Wimbledon when it rains) and move the carpets from one heap to another; and what was on the top now goes to the bottom. Find out the times of the turning and be there to watch, or else you might miss something crucial, While the porters are doing the turning, you can stand there armed with a catalogue and make some scribbled notes. If you want to inspect any carpet while they are being turned, simply ask them to pause while you have a careful look.

When I went to the sale with my clients Olga and Olga they had looked at the catalogue and decided that they were keen on a certain very large rug that happened to be at the bottom of the pile. When they came to inspect it, they found that there was a huge hole in the middle. It so happened that we found that at this time traditional designs, such as Persian rugs with wonderful intricate patterns and highly colourful woven rugs, are not that fashionable because of the interior designer business – predominantly in America and in Europe – pushing the market-place to a minimalist look. The prices of Oriental carpets and rugs reflect trends in decorating, so this proved to be one of the occasions when what I call 'the curse of the designer' can work for the buyer. Much to their pleasure and surprise, the two Olgas were able to get the rug of their dreams for £400, probably a tenth of what it might have cost a year or two back. They were so delighted that they bought two rugs; but I should point out that they didn't buy the second on a whim – they had previously inspected it.

What goes around comes around, and sooner or later a particular look – in this case, the traditional carpet – will come back again and the price will soar. I think the same is probably so with furniture and with certain objects of art, which also become fashionable, or go out of fashion through interior decorators, designers and magazines, all showing the public what's 'in', rather as fashion designers state that this year's colour is grey or pink.

Buying at Auction – on Line

AN OLD TRADITIONALIST like me finds computers and the Internet a complete mystery. But let's face it, there is no doubt it is the future of retailing. At the time of writing even the venerable house of Sotheby's is now holding auctions on the Internet! But be warned: auctions on the Internet can be great fun but the opportunities for fraud are huge and you should be very careful.

So how do they work?

THE PRINCIPLE is the same on all auction web sites. You register, you are given a secure access code, which only you know, and away you go. Each item is auctioned from a particular time and date and proceeds for a set amount of time. If you have any questions not answered in the descriptions, you e-mail the seller before committing to a bid. There may or may not be a reserve and there may be increments which you have to bid in. If your bid is exceeded most sites have a mechanism whereby the computer automatically e-mails you the new bid and asks if you want to continue. At the end of the auction, the venue will exchange e-mail addresses of the seller and highest bidder. The seller and buyer then contact each other to get the appropriate address information in order to exchange the payment and merchandise.

ONLINE AUCTIONS can be a fun way to shop, but remember that it is important to practise safe buying and selling when you are online. Just like real auctions, 'virtual' actions have their dos and don'ts. Use caution and common sense. The most common major problems are with merchandise undelivered, items misrepresented and defective or damaged goods. Ask yourself: is what the seller promises realistic? Is this the best way to buy this item? What is the most I am willing to bid for it? Reputable auction houses such as Sotheby's have their reputations to consider and they auction goods with all the guarantees they would give in a real auction.

The following tips, should help:

FIRST THERE'S the obvious one: you cannot actually handle and see for yourself what you are buying. Sure, on some web sites you can zoom in and move around the object, but like looking in a catalogue you cannot see the blemishes, bumps and bashes.

UNDERSTAND how the auction works. Go through the instructions on the web site carefully. Use the e-mail enquiry service if you have any questions.

MANY ON-LINE auctions simply list items that people want to sell. They don't verify if the merchandise actually exists or is described accurately. Remember that auction web sites are merely 'venues' therefore, if you feel at all unsure about a transaction, ask the seller to put the item and payment with a third party who can verify the item is what it is supposed to be and that the money is paid. Some venues are able to offer such an 'escrow service'.

CHECK OUT the seller. If the seller is based in the United States contact the local consumer protection agency in the appropriate state. Look at the auction site's feedback section for comments about the seller. Look out for bogus comments from the seller themselves.

BE ESPECIALLY careful if the seller is a private individual. It's very difficult to track down individuals who abscond. Get a physical address and other identifying information from the seller. Don't do business with sellers who won't provide that information.

SINCE YOU can't examine the item or have it appraised until after the sale, you can't assume that claims made about it are valid. Insist on getting a written statement describing the item and its value before you pay.

IF YOU WIN the auction the buyer should ask about delivery, returns, warranties and service. Get a definite delivery time and insist that the shipment be insured. Ask about the return policy. If you're buying electronic goods or appliances, find out if there is a warranty and how to get service. Sellers usually include their payment and delivery terms in the description of the product.

PAY THE safest way. Requesting cash is a clear sign of fraud. If possible, pay by credit card because you can dispute the charges if the goods are misrepresented or never arrive. Or use an escrow agent, who acts as a go-between to receive the merchandise and forward your payment to the seller. Another option is cash on delivery (COD). Pay by cheque made out to the seller, so you can stop payment if necessary.

LOOK ON the World Wide Web for the Internet Fraud Watch site (www.fraud.org/ifw.htm). This will give you other tips about buying safely over the net.

FOR ONLINE auctions try:
ebay.co.uk
icollector.com
sothebys.com
christies.com
amazon.co.uk

or for more information about antiques:
antiquesworld.co.uk
antiquesroadshow.co.uk

Guide for Prospective Buyers

The following extract is an abbreviated version of Sotheby's *Important Information for Buyers* and does not contain certain details and references which would normally appear. This information can be found in Sotheby's sale catalogues. Similar guides can be found in all auction sale catalogues.

HOW TO BUY AT AUCTION

The following pages are designed to give you useful information on how to buy at auction. Sotheby's staff as listed at the front of this catalogue under Sales Enquiries and Information will be happy to assist you. If you have not bought at Sotheby's recently, it is important that you read the following information carefully.

PROVENANCE

In certain circumstances, Sotheby's may print in the catalogue the history of ownership of a work of art if such information contributes to scholarship or is otherwise well known and assists in distinguishing the work of art. However, the identity of the seller or previous owners may not be disclosed for a variety of reasons. For example, such information may be excluded to accommodate a seller's request for confidentiality or because the identity of prior owners is unknown given the age of the work of art.

BUYER'S PREMIUM

With the exception of Wine and Coins, a buyer's premium is payable by the buyer of each lot at a rate of 15 per cent on the first £30,000 of the hammer price of the lot and at a rate of 10 per cent on the amount by which the hammer price of the lot exceeds £30,000. For Wine and Coins, a buyer's premium of 10 per cent of the hammer price is payable by the buyer of each lot.

VAT

Value Added Tax (VAT) may be payable on the hammer price and/or the buyer's premium. Buyer's premium may attract a charge in lieu of VAT.

1. BEFORE THE AUCTION

CATALOGUE SUBSCRIPTIONS AND SOTHEBY'S SEARCH SERVICES

Annual subscriptions to catalogues will ensure that you receive catalogues regularly.

PRE-SALE ESTIMATES

The pre-sale estimates are intended as a guide for prospective buyers. Any bid between the high and the low pre-sale estimates would, in our opinion, offer a fair chance of success. However, all lots, depending on the degree of competition, can realise prices either above or below the pre-sale estimates.

It is always advisable to consult us nearer the time of sale as estimates can be subject to revision. The estimates printed in the auction catalogue do not include the buyer's premium or VAT.

PRE-SALE ESTIMATES IN US DOLLARS AND EUROS

Although the sale is conducted in pounds sterling, for your convenience, the pre-sale estimates in some catalogues are also printed in US dollars and/or Euros. The rate of exchange from pound sterling to US dollar and/or Euro is the rate at the time of production of this catalogue. The rate of exchange will have changed between the time of production of the catalogue and the time of the sale. Therefore, you should not treat the estimates in US dollars or Euros as anything other than an approximation of the estimates in pounds sterling.

CONDITION OF LOTS

Prospective buyers are encouraged to inspect the property at the pre-sale exhibitions. Solely as a convenience, Sotheby's may provide condition reports. The absence of reference to the condition of a lot in the catalogue description does not imply that the lot is free from faults or imperfections.

ELECTRICAL AND MECHANICAL GOODS

All electrical and mechanical goods are sold on the basis of their decorative value only and should not be assumed to be operative. It is essential that prior to any intended use, the electrical system is checked and approved by a qualified electrician.

2. BIDDING IN THE SALE

BIDDING AT AUCTION

Bids may be executed in person by paddle during the auction, in writing prior to the sale or by telephone. All auctions are conducted in pounds sterling.

Auction speeds vary, but usually average 50–120 lots per hour. The bidding steps are generally in increments of approximately 10 per cent of the previous bid.

BIDDING IN PERSON

To bid in person at the auction, you will need to register for and collect a numbered paddle before the auction begins. Proof of identity will be required. If you have a Sotheby's Identification Card, it will facilitate the registration process.

The paddle is used to indicate your bids to the auctioneer during the sale. Should you be the successful buyer of any lot, please ensure that your paddle can be seen by the auctioneer and that it is your number that is called out. Should there be any doubts as to price or buyer, please draw the auctioneer's attention to it immediately.

All lots sold will be invoiced to the name and address in which the paddle has been registered and cannot be transferred to other names and addresses.

Please do not mislay your paddle; in the event of loss, please inform the Sales Clerk immediately. At the end of the sale, please return your paddle to the registration desk.

ABSENTEE BIDS

If you cannot attend the auction, we will be happy to execute written bids on your behalf. A bidding form can be found at the back of this catalogue. This service is free and confidential. Lots will always be bought as cheaply as is consistent with other bids, the reserves and Sotheby's commissions. In the event of identical bids, the earliest bid received will take precedence. Always indicate a 'top limit' – the hammer price to which you would bid if you were attending the auction yourself. 'Buy' and unlimited bids will not be accepted.

Telephoned absentee bids must be confirmed before the sale by letter or fax.

To ensure a satisfactory service to bidders, please ensure that we receive your bids at least 24 hours before the sale.

BIDDING BY TELEPHONE

If you cannot attend the auction, it is possible to bid on the telephone on lots with a minimum low estimate of £1,000. As the number of telephone lines is limited, it is necessary to make arrangements for this service 24 hours before the sale.

We also suggest that you leave a maximum bid which we can execute on your behalf in the event we are unable to reach you by telephone. Multi-lingual staff are available to execute bids for you.

EMPLOYEE BIDDING

Sotheby's employees may bid in a Sotheby's auction only if the employee does not know the reserve and if the employee fully complies with Sotheby's internal rules governing employee bidding.

UN EMBARGO ON TRADE WITH IRAQ
[AS OF PUBLICATION DATE]

The United Nations trade embargo prohibits us from accepting bids from any person in Iraq (including any body controlled by Iraqi residents or companies, wherever carrying on business), or from any other person where we have reasonable cause to believe (i) that the lot(s) will be supplied or delivered to or to the order of a person in Iraq or (ii) that the lot(s) will be used for the purposes of any business carried on in or operated from Iraq. Acceptance of bids by the auctioneer is subject to this prohibition.

For further details, please contact a member of the Expert Department or the Legal Department PRIOR to bidding.

3. THE AUCTION

CONDITIONS OF BUSINESS

The auction is governed by the Conditions of Business printed in this catalogue. These Conditions of Business apply to all aspects of the relationship between Sotheby's and actual and prospective bidders and buyers. Anyone considering bidding in the auction should read them carefully. They may be amended by way of notices posted in the saleroom or by way of announcement made by the auctioneer.

CONSECUTIVE AND RESPONSIVE BIDDING

The auctioneer may open the bidding on any lot by placing a bid on behalf of the seller.

The auctioneer may further bid on behalf of the seller, up to the amount of the reserve, by placing consecutive or responsive bids for a lot.

4. AFTER THE AUCTION

PAYMENT

Payment is due immediately after the sale.

The Conditions of Business require buyers to pay immediately for their purchases. However, in limited circumstances and generally with the seller's agreement, Sotheby's may offer buyers it deems credit worthy the option of paying for their purchases on an extended payment term basis. Generally credit terms must be arranged prior to the Sale. In advance of determining whether to grant the extended payment terms, Sotheby's may require credit references and proof of identity and residence.

COLLECTION

Lots will be released to you or your authorised representative when full and cleared payment has been received by Sotheby's and a release note has been produced by our Cashiers at New Bond Street.

Smaller items can normally be collected from the Packing Room at New Bond Street, however large items will be sent to Sotheby's Kings House Warehouse.

If you are in any doubt about the location of your purchases, please contact the Sale Administrator prior to arranging collection. Removal, interest, storage and handling charges will be levied on uncollected lots.

STORAGE AND HANDLING

Storage and handling charges plus VAT may apply.

INSURANCE

Buyers are reminded that lots are only insured for a maximum of five (5) working days after the day of the auction.

DESPATCH AND TRANSIT INSURANCE

Purchases will be dispatched as soon as possible upon clearance from the Accounts Department and receipt of your written despatch instructions and of any export licence or certificates that may be required. Despatch will be arranged at the buyer's expense. Sotheby's may receive a fee for its own account from the agent arranging despatch. Estimates and information on all methods can be provided upon request and enquiries should be marked for the attention of Sotheby's Shipping Department.

Insurance cover will be arranged for property in transit unless otherwise specified in writing and will be at the buyer's expense. All shipments should be unpacked and checked on delivery and any discrepancies notified to the Transit insurer or shipper immediately.

A form to provide shipping instructions is usually printed on the reverse of the bid slip printed in the catalogue or on the back of your buyers invoice.

EXPORT

The export of any lot from the UK or import into any other country may be subject to one or more export or import licences being granted. It is the buyer's responsibility to obtain any relevant export or import licence. Buyers are reminded that lots purchased must be paid for immediately after the auction. The denial of any export or import licence required or any delay in obtaining such licence cannot justify the cancellation of the sale or any delay in making payment of the total amount due.

Sotheby's, upon request, may apply for a licence to export your lot(s) outside the United Kingdom.

An EU Licence is necessary to export from the European Community cultural goods subject to the EU Regulation on the export of cultural property (EEC No. 3911/92, Official Journal No. L395 of 31/12/92.

A UK Licence is necessary to move from the UK to another Member State of the EU cultural goods valued at or above the relevant UK licence limit. A UK Licence may also be necessary to export outside the European Community cultural goods valued at or above the relevant UK licence limit but below the EU licence limit.

The following is a selection of some of the categories and a summary of the limits above which either an EU or a UK Licence may be required for items more than 50 years old:-

Paintings in oil or tempera	£119,000
Watercolours	£23,800
Prints, Drawings & Engravings	£11,900
British Historical Portraits	£6,000
Photographs	£6,000
Arms and Armour	£20,000
Textiles	£6,000
Printed Maps	£11,900
Books	£39,600
Any Other Objects	£39,600
Manuscripts/Archives/Scale Drawings	*
Archaeological items	*

(* a licence will be required in most instances, irrespective of value)

EXPORT TO ITALY

Buyers intending to export their purchases to Italy under an Italian Temporary Cultural Import Licence are advised that the Italian authorities will require evidence of export from the UK.

ENDANGERED SPECIES

Items made of or incorporating animal material such as ivory; whale bone; tortoise-shell etc., irrespective of age or value, require a specific licence from the Department of the Environment, prior to leaving the UK. Sotheby's suggests that buyers also check with their own relevant government department regarding the importation of such items.

EMBARGO ON IMPORTATION OF PERSIAN/IRANIAN WORKS OF ART AND CARPETS IN TO THE U.S.A.

Clients considering purchasing Persian/Iranian works of art or carpets with the intention of exporting them to the U.S.A., should enquire with the relevant U.S. Government Office regarding the proper importation of such items into the U.S. prior to shipping the lot(s) to the U.S.

5. ADDITIONAL SERVICES

PRE-SALE AUCTION ESTIMATES

Sotheby's will be pleased to give preliminary pre-sale auction estimates for your property. This service is free of charge and is available from Sotheby's experts in New Bond Street on week days between 9 am and 4.30 pm. We advise you to make an appointment with the relevant expert department. We will inspect your property and advise you without charge. Upon request, we may also travel to your home to provide preliminary pre-sale auction estimates.

VALUATIONS

The Valuation department provides written inventories and valuations throughout Europe for many purposes including insurance, probate and succession, asset management and tax planning. Valuations can be tailored to suit most needs.

TAX AND HERITAGE ADVICE

Our Tax and Heritage department provides advice on the tax implications of sales and related legal and heritage issues. It can also assist in private treaty sales, on transfers in lieu of taxation, on the obtaining of conditional exemption from tax and on UK export issues.

Where to Look

This is a guide to some of the
main auction houses, salerooms,
antiques fairs and markets
in the England, Scotland and
Wales, with details of where
they are and when they happen.
Wherever you are, there is a
bargain to be found!

Every effort has been made
to ensure that the details are
correct at the time of going
to press, but it is advisable to
double check before setting out.

AUCTION HOUSES AND SALEROOMS

LONDON

Academy Auctioneers & Valuers
Northcote House
Northcote Avenue
Ealing
London
W5 3UR
Tel: 020 8579 7466
www.thesaurus.co.uk/academy

Bloomsbury Book Auctions
3-4 Hardwick Street
London
EC1R 4RY
Tel: 020 7833 2636/7
www.bloomsbury-book-auct.com

Bonhams Chelsea
65-69 Lots Road
Chelsea
London
SW10 0RN
Tel: 020 7393 3900
www.bonhams.com

Bonhams Knightsbridge
Montpelier Street
Knightsbridge
London
SW7 1HH
Tel: 020 7393 3900
www.bonhams.com

Chiswick Auctions
1 Colville Road
London
W3
Tel: 020 8992 4442

Christie's
8 King Street
St James's
London
SW1Y 6QT
Tel: 020 7839 9060
www.christies.com

Christie's – South Kensington
85 Old Brompton Road
London
SW7 3LD
Tel: 020 7581 7611
www.christies.com

Criterion Auctioneers
53 Essex Road
Islington
London
N1
Tel: 020 7359 5007
www.criterion-auctioneers.co.uk

Dix Noonan Webb
1 Old Bond Street
London
W1X 3TD
Tel: 020 7499 5022
auction@dnw.co.uk

Forrest & Co. Ltd
Lancaster House
Lancaster Road
Leytonstone
London
E11
Tel: 020 8534 2931

Stanley Gibbons Auctions Ltd
399 Strand
London
WC2R OLX
Tel: 020 7836 8444
auctions@stangiblondon.demon.co.uk

Glendining & Co.
101 New Bond Street
London
W1F 1SR
Tel: 020 7493 2445

Harmers of London Stamp Auctioneers Ltd
111 Power Road
Chiswick
London
W4 5PY
Tel: 020 8747 6100

Hornsey Auctions Ltd
54-56 High Street
Hornsey
London
N8 7NX
Tel: 020 8340 5334

Lloyds International Auction Galleries Ltd
118 Putney Bridge Road
Putney
London
SW15 2NQ
Tel: 020 8788 7777
www.lloyds-auction.co.uk

Lots Road Galleries
71-73 Lots Road
Chelsea
London
SW10 0RN
Tel: 020 7376 6800
www.auctions-on-line.com/lotsroad

Nash & Co.
Lodge House
9-17 Lodge Lande
London
N12
Tel: 0208 445 9000

Phillips International Auctioneers & Valuers
Head Office & International
Saleroom
101 New Bond St
London
W1Y 9LG
Tel: 020 7629 6602
www.phillips-auction.com

Phillips International Auctioneers & Valuers
Bayswater Saleroom
10 Salem Rd
London
W2 4DL
Tel: 020 7229 9090
www.phillips.auction.com

Rippon Boswell & Co.
The Arcade
South Kensington Station
London
SW7 2NA
Tel: 020 7589 4242

Rosebery Fine Art
74-76 Knights Hill
West Norwood
London
SE27 0JD
Tel: 020 8761 2522

Sotheby's
34-35 New Bond Street
London
W1A 2AA
Tel: 020 7293 5000

Southgate Auction Rooms
55 High Street
Southgate
London
N14 6LD
Tel: 020 8886 7888

Thornwood Auctions
Thornwood Village Hall
Weald Hall Lane
Thornwood
Epping
London
E18
Tel: 020 8553 1242

Woodford Auctions
209 High Road
South Woodford
London
E18
Tel: 020 8553 1242

BEDFORDSHIRE

BBG Wilson Peacock
The Auction Centre
26 Newnham Street
Bedford
MK40 3JR
Tel: 01234 266366

Douglas Ross Auctioneers
The Old Town Hall
Woburn
MK17 9PZ
Tel: 01525 290502

BERKSHIRE

Dreweatt Neate
Donnington Priory
Donnington
Nr Newbury
RG14 2JE
Tel: 01635 553553
www.dreweatt-neate.co.uk

Edwards & Elliott
32 High Street
Ascot
SL5 7HG
Tel: 01344 625022
www.edwardsandelliott.co.uk

Martin & Pole Nicholas
The Auction House
Milton Road
Wokingham
RG40 1DB
Tel: 0118 979 0460
www.martinpole.co.uk

Thimbleby & Shorland
31 Great Knollys Street
Reading
RG1 7HU
Tel: 0118 950 8611

BUCKINGHAMSHIRE

Amersham Auction Rooms
125 Station Road
Amersham
HP7 OAH
Tel: 01494 729292

Old Amersham Auctions
2 School Lane
Amersham
Buckinghamshire
HP7 OEL
Tel: 01494 722758

CAMBRIDGESHIRE

BBG Wilson Peacock
The Auction Centre
75 New Street
St Neots
PE19 1AN
Tel: 01480 474550

Cheffins, Grain & Comins
The Cambridge Saleroom
2 Clifton Road
Cambridge
CB1 4BW
Tel: 01223 213343
www.cheffins.co.uk

Goldsmiths
15 Market Place
Oundle
Peterborough
PE8 4BA
Tel: 01832 272349

Grounds & Co.
2 Nene Quay
Wisbech
PE13 1AQ
Tel: 01945 585041

Hyperion Auction Centre
Station Road
St Ives
Huntingdon
PE17 4BH
Tel: 01480 464140
hyperion-auctions@hotmail.com

**Phillips International
Auctioneers & Valuers**
The Golden Rose
17 Emmanuel Rd
Cambridge
CB1 1JW
Tel: 01223 366523
www.phillips-auction.com

CHESHIRE

Andrew, Hilditch & Son Ltd
Hanover House
1a The Square
Sandbach
CW11 OAP
Tel: 01270 767246

John Arnold & Co.
Central Salerooms
15 Station Road
Cheadle Hulme
SK8 5AF
Tel: 0161 485 2777

Patrick Cheyne
38 Hale Road
Altrincham
WA14 2EX
Tel: 0161 941 4879

Halls Fine Art Ltd
Booth Mansion
30 Watergate Street
Chester
CH1 2LA
Tel: 01244 312300
www.halls-auctioneers.ltd.uk

Frank R. Marshall & Co.
Marshall House
Church Hill
Knutsford
WA16 6DH
Tel: 01565 653284
www.thesaurus.co.uk

**Phillips International
Auctioneers & Valuers –
North West**
New House
150 Christleton Road
Chester
CH3 5TD
Tel: 01244 313936
www.phillips-auction.com

**Peter Wilson Fine Art
Auctioneers**
Victoria Gallery
Market Street
Nantwich
CW5 5DG
Tel: 01270 623878
www.peterwilson.co.uk

Wright Manley Auctioneers
Beeston Castle Salerooms
Beeston
Tarporley
CW6 ODR
Tel: 01829 260767

Cornwall

Helston Auction Rooms
5 The Parade
Trengrouse Way
Helston
Tel: 01326 563640
auctionhar@aol.com

Jefferys
The Auction Rooms
5 Fore Street
Lostwithiel
PL22 OBP
Tel: 01208 872245
jefferys.lostwithiel@btinternet.com

Lambrays
Polmoria Walk Galleries
The Platt
Wadebridge
PL27 7AE
Tel: 01208 813593

W.H.Lane & Son Fine Art Auctioneers & Valuers
Jubilee House
Queen Street
Penzance
TR18 4DF
Tel: 011736 361447
graham.bazley@excite.com

David Lay
The Penzance Auction House
Alverton
Penzance
TR18 4RE
Tel: 01736 361414
www.catalogs.icollector.com/dlay

Pearce & Richards
The Old Chapel
Mount Street
Penzance
Tel: 01736 363816

Phillips International Auctioneers & Valuers – Cornwall
Cornubia Hall
Eastcliffe Road
Par
PL24 2AQ
Tel: 01726 814047
www.phillips-auction.com

Martyn Rowe Auctioneers & Valuers
The Truro Auction Centre
City Wharf
Malpas Road
Truro
TR1 1QH
Tel: 01872 260020

Cumbria

Bonhams
Cook House
Church Road
Levens
Kendal
Tel: 01539 560699
www.bonhams.com

Cumbria Auction Rooms
12 Lowther Street
Carlisle
CA3 8DA
Tel: 01228 525259

Cumbria Auction Rooms
Rosehill Saleroom
Carlisle
CA1 2RS
Tel: 01228 640927

Gedyes Auctioneers & Estate Agents
The Auction Centre
Main Street
Grange over Sands
LA11 6AB
Tel: 015395 33316
gedyes@aol.com

Mitchell's Auction Co.
The Furniture Hall
47 Station Road
Cockermouth
CA13 9PZ
Tel: 01900 827800
www.mitchellsauction.co.uk

Penrith Farmers' & Kidds Plc
Skirsgill Saleroom
Skirsgill
Penrith
CA11 ODN
Tel: 01768 890781
www.collector.com

**Phillips International
Auctioneers & Valuers**
48 Cecil Street
Carlisle
CA1 1NT
Tel: 01228 542422
www.phillips-auction.com

James Thompson
64 Main Street
Kirkby Lonsdale
LA6 2AJ
Tel: 015242 71555

**Thomson, Roddick & Laurie
Ltd**
19 Crosby Street
Carlisle
CA1 1DQ
Tel: 01228 528939

DERBYSHIRE

Armstrong Auctions
Midland Road
Swadlincote
DE11 OAH
Tel: 01283 217772

Neales Auctioneers
Becket Street
Derby
DE1 1HU
Tel: 01332 295543

Noel Wheatcroft & Son
Matlock Auction Gallery
The Old Picture Palace
Dale Road
Matlock
DE4 3LU
Tel: 01629 57460
www.wheatcroft-noel.co.uk

DEVON

Bearne's
St Edmund's Court
Okehampton Street
Exeter
EX4 1DU
Tel: 01392 207000
www.auctions-on-line.com/bearnes

Bonhams West Country
Dowell Street
Honiton
EX14 1LX
Tel: 01404 41872
www.bonhams.com

Kingsbridge Auction Sales
Market Hall
113 Fore Street
Kingsbridge
TQ7 1BG
Tel: 01364 531439

Lyme-Bay Auction Galleries
28 Harbour Road
Seaton
EX12 2NA
Tel: 01297 22453

**Phillips International
Auctioneers & Valuers**
Alphin Brook Road
Alphington
Exeter
EX2 8TH
Tel: 01392 439025
www.phillips-auction.com

Plymouth Auction Rooms
Edwin House
St Johns Road
Cattedown
Plymouth
PL4 ONZ
Tel: 01752 254 740
paulkeen@plymouthauctions.freeserve
.co.uk

Potbury & Sons
The Auction Rooms
Temple Street
Sidmouth
EX10 8LN
Tel: 01395 515555/517300

Rendells
Stone Park
Ashburton
TQ13 7RH
Tel: 01364 653017
www.rendells.co.uk

Taylor's
Honiton Galleries
205 High Street
Honiton
EX14 1LQ
Tel: 01404 42404
www.thesaurus.co.uk/taylors

**Ward & Chowen Auction
Rooms**
Market Road
Tavistock
PL19 OBW
Tel: 01822 612603

Whitton & Laing
32 Okehampton Street
Exeter
EX4 1DY
Tel: 01392 496607

DORSET

The Auction House Bridport
38a St Michael Trading Estate
Bridport
DT6 3RR
Tel: 01308 459400
enquiries@theauctionhouse.dabsol.co.
uk

Cottees
The Market
East Street
Wareham
BH20 4NR
Tel: 01929 552826
www.btinternet.com/~cotteesauction
rooms

Hy. Duke & Son
Dorchester Fine Art Salerooms
Weymouth Avenue
Dorchester
DT1 1QS
Tel: 01305 265080

Hy. Duke & Son
The Weymouth Salerooms
Nicholas Street
Weymouth
DT4 8AA
Tel: 01305 761499

House & Son
Lansdowne House
Christchurch Road
Bournemouth
BH1 3JW
Tel: 01202 298044

William Morey & Sons
Salerooms
St Michaels Lane
Bridport
DT6 3RB
Tel: 01308 422078

Phillips Auctioneers
Gild House
70 Norwich Avenue
West Bournemouth
BH2 6AW
Tel: 01202 769352/01935 815271

Phillips International Auctioneers & Valuers
3 Cheap Street
Sherborne
DT9 3PT
Tel: 01935 815271
www.phillips-auction.com

Riddetts of Bournemouth
177 Holdenhurst Road
Bournemouth
BH8 8DQ
Tel: 01202 555686
auctions@riddetts.co.uk

Southern Counties Auctioneers
The Livestock Market
Christys Lane
Shaftesbury
SP7 8PH
Tel: 01747 851735

DURHAM

Denis Edkins
Auckland Auction Rooms
58 Kingsway
Bishop Auckland
DL14 7JF
Tel: 01388 603095

G. Tarn Bainbridge & Son
Northern Rock House
High Row
Darlington
DL3 7QN
Tel: 01325 462633

Thomas Watson & Son
Northumberland Street
Darlington
DL3 7HJ
Tel: 01323 462559

ESSEX

BBG Ambrose
Ambrose House
Old Station Road
Loughton
IG10 4PE
Tel: 020 8502 3951

Chalkwell Auctions Ltd
The Arlington Rooms
905 London Road
Leigh-on-Sea
SS0 8NU
Tel: 01702 710383

Cooper Hirst Auctions
The Granary Salerooms
Victoria Road
Chelmsford
CM2 6LH
Tel: 01245 260535

Reeman Dansie Howe & Son
Head Gate Auction Rooms
12 Head Gate
Colchester
CO3 3BT
Tel: 01206 574271

Simon H. Rowland
Chelmsford Auction Rooms
42 Mildmay Road
Chelmsford
CM2 ODZ
Tel: 01245 354251

Saffron Walden Auctions
1 Market Street
Saffron Walden
CB10 1JB
Tel: 01799 513281

John Stacey & Sons Ltd
Leigh Auction Rooms
86-90 Pall Mall
Leigh-on-Sea
SS9 1RG
Tel: 01702 477051
jstacey@easynet.co.uk

Stanfords
11-14 East Hill
Colchester
CO1 2QX
Tel: 01206 868070

G. E. Sworder & Sons
14 Cambridge Road
Stansted
CM24 8BZ
Tel: 01279 817778
www.auctions-online.com/sworder

Trembath Welch
Old Town Hall
Great Dunmow
CM6 1AU
Tel: 01371 873014
www.thesaurus.co.uk/dtrembath/

GLOUCESTERSHIRE

BK The Property Assets Consultancy
Albion Chambers
111 Eastgate Street
Gloucester
GL1 1PZ
Tel: 01452 521 267
www.bkonline.co.uk

Bristol Auction Rooms Ltd
St John's Place
Apsley Road
Clifton
Bristol
BS8 2ST
Tel: 0117 973 7201

Corinium Galleries
25 Gloucester Street
Cirencester
GL7 2DJ
Tel: 01285 659057

The Cotswold Auction Co. Ltd
Chapel Walk Saleroom
Chapel Walk
Cheltenham
GL50 3DS
Tel: 01242 256363

Fraser Glennie & Partners
The Coach House
Upper Siddington
Cirencester
GL7 6HL
Tel: 01285 659677

Mallams Fine Art Auctioneers & Valuers
Grosvenor Galleries
26 Grosvenor Street
Cheltenham
GL52 2SG
Tel: 01242 235712
www.thesaurus.co.uk/mallams

Moore Allen & Innocent
33 Castle Street
Cirencester
GL7 1QD
Tel: 01285 651831

Short, Graham & Co.
City Chambers
4-6 Clarence Street
Gloucester
GL1 1DX
Tel: 01452 521177

Wotton Auction Rooms Ltd
Tabernacle Road
Wotton-under-Edge
GL12 7EB
Tel: 01453 844733
wotton_auction.rooms@compuserve.
com

HAMPSHIRE

Andover Saleroom
41a London Street
Andover
SP10 2NU
Tel: 01264 364820

**Jacobs & Hunt Fine Art
Auctioneers**
26 Lavant Street
Petersfield
GU32 3EF
Tel: 01730 233933
www.jacobsandhunt.co.uk

George Kidner Auctioneers
The Old School
The Square
Pennington
Lymington
SO41 8GN
Tel: 01590 670070
commissions@gkidner.freeserve.co.uk

May & Son
18 Bridge Street
Andover
SP10 1BH
Tel: 01264 323417/363331
mayandson@enterprise.net

D. M. Nesbit & Co.
7 Clarendon Road
Southsea
Portsmouth
PO5 2ED
Tel: 023 9286 4321
nesbits@compuserve.com

**Phillips International
Auctioneers & Valuers**
54 Southampton Road
Ringwood
BH24 1JD
Tel: 01425 473333
www.phillips-auction.com

**Phillips International
Auctioneers & Valuers**
The Red House
Hyde Street
Winchester
SO23 7DX
Tel:01962 862515
www.phillips-auction.com

Romsey Auction Rooms
86 The Hundred
Romsey
SO51 8BX
Tel: 01794 513331

HEREFORDSHIRE

Russell, Baldwin & Bright
The Fine Art Saleroom
Ryelands Road
Leominster
HR6 8NZ
Tel: 01568 611122
www.catalogs.icollector.com/russell

Sunderlands Salerooms
Cattle Market
Newmarket Street
Hereford
HR4 9HX
Tel: 01432 266894

HERTFORDSHIRE

Berkhamstead Auction Rooms
Middle Road
Berkhamstead
HP4 3EQ
Tel: 01442 865169

Brown and Merry
Tring Market Auctions
Brook Street
Tring
HP23 5EF
Tel: 01442 826446

ISLE OF WIGHT

Shanklin Auction Rooms
79 Regent Street
Shanklin
PO37 7AP
Tel: 01983 863441
shanklin.auction@tesco.net

Ways
The Auction House
Garfield Road
Ryde
PO33 2PT
Tel: 01983 562255

KENT

Bracketts Fine Art Auctioneers
Auction Hall
Pantiles
Tunbridge Wells
TN2 5QL
Tel: 01892 544500

The Canterbury Auction Galleries
40 Station Road
West Canterbury
CT2 8AN
Tel: 01227 763337

Halifax Property Services – Fine Art Department
15 Cattle Market
Sandwich
CT13 9AW
Tel: 01304 614369

Hobbs Parker
Romney House
Ashford Market
Orbital Park
Ashford
TN24 OHB
Tel: 01233 502222
www.hobbsparker.co.uk

Hogben Fine Art Auctioneers & Valuers
Unit C Highfield Industrial Estate
Warren Road
Folkestone
CT19 6DD
Tel: 01303 246810
www.catalogs.icollector.com/hogben

Ibbett Mosely
125 High Street
Sevenoaks
TN13 1UT
Tel: 01732 456731

Lambert & Foster Auction Sale Rooms
102 High Street
Tenterden
TN30 6HU
Tel: 01580 762083
Lambert.Foster@Farmline.com

B. J. Norris
The Quest
West Street
Harrietsham
ME17 1JD
Tel: 01622 859515
www.antiquesbulletin.com/bjnorris

Phillips International Auctioneers & Valuers
49 London Rd
Sevenoaks
TN13 1AR
Tel: 01732 740310
www.phillips-auction.com

Stabledoors & Co.
94-98 High Street
Beckenham
BR3 1ED
Tel: 020 8650 9270

LANCASHIRE

Acorn Philatelic Auctions
PO Box 152
Salford
Manchester
M17 1BP
Tel: 0161 877 8818

The Auction Galleries
38 Charles Street
Manchester
M1 7DB
Tel: 0161 273 1911
www.catalogs.icollector.com/capesdum

**Capes Dunn & Co. Fine Art
Auctioneers & Valuers**
Central Auction Rooms
4 Baron Street
Rochdale
OL16 1SJ
Tel: 01706 646298

Kingsway Auction Rooms Ltd
The Galleries
Kingsway
Ansdell
Lytham St Annes
FY8 1AB
Tel: 01253 735442

Warren & Wignall Ltd
The Mill
Earnshaw Bridge
Leyland
PR5 3PH
Tel: 01772 451430

LEICESTERSHIRE

Churchgate Auctions Ltd
66 Churchgate
Leicester
LE1 4AL
Tel: 01162 621416
www.churchgateauctions.co.uk

Freckeltons
1 Leicester Road
Loughborough
LE11 2AE
Tel: 01509 214564

Gilding's Auctioneers & Valuers
Roman Way
Markey Harborough
LE16 7PQ
Tel: 01858 410414

Heathcote Ball & Co.
Castle Auction Rooms
78 St Nicholas Circle
Leicester
LE1 5NW
Tel: 0116 2536789
hcb@ball2000.fsnet.co.uk

LINCOLNSHIRE

DDM Auction Rooms Ltd
Old Court Road
Brigg
DN20 8JJ
Tel: 01652 650172
www.ddmgroup.co.uk

Dowse
Foresters' Galleries
Falkland Way
Barton-upon-Humber
DN18 5RL
Tel: 01652 632 335

Eleys Auctioneers
210 Wide Bargate
Boston
PE21 6RR
Tel: 01205 361687

Escritt & Barrell Saleroom
Dysart Road
Grantham
NG31 6QF
Tel: 01476 566991

Golding, Young & Co.
The Grantham Auction Rooms
Old Wharf Road
Grantham
NG31 7AA
Tel: 01476 565118
www.thesaurus.co.uk/gy&c

Thomas Mawer & Son
63 Monks Road
Lincoln
LN2 5HP
Tel: 01522 524984
mawer.thos@lineone.net

Richardsons
Bourne Auction Rooms
Spalding Road
Bourne
PE10 9LE
Tel: 01778 422686

Marilyn Swain Auctions
The Old Barracks
Sandon Road
Grantham
NG31 9AS
Tel: 01476 568861
www.swainsauctions.co.uk

MERSEYSIDE

Abram & Mitchell
41 Stanhope Street
Liverpool
L8 5RF
Tel: 0151 708 5180

J. Kent (Auctioneers) Ltd
2-6 Valkyrie Road
Wallasey
L46 4RQ
Tel: 0151 638 3107

Kingsley & Co. Auctioneers
3-4 The Quadrant
Hoylake
Worral
L47 2EE
Tel: 0151 632 5821
kingsleyauctions@msn.com

Outhwaite & Litherland
Kingsway Galleries
Fontenoy Street
Liverpool
L3 2BE
Tel: 0151 236 6561
www.lots.uk.com

NORFOLK

Beck Auctions
The Cornhall
Cattle Market Street
Fakenham
NR21 9AW
Tel: 01328 851557

Clowes Nash Auctions
Norwich Livestock &
Commercial Centre
Hall Road
Norwich
NR4 6EQ
Tel: 01603 504488

Ewings
Market Place
Reepham
Norwich
NR10 4JJ
Tel: 01603 870473

Thos. Wm Gaze & Son
Diss Auction Rooms
Roydon Road
Diss
IP22 4LN
Tel: 01379 650306
www.twgaze.com

Great Yarmouth Salerooms
Beaver Road
Great Yarmouth
NR30 3PS
Tel: 01493 332668

**G.A. Key Auctioneers
& Valuers**
Aylsham Salerooms
8 Market Place
Aylsham
NR11 6EH
Tel: 01263 733195

NORTHAMPTONSHIRE

Goldsmiths
15 Market Place
Oundle
PE8 4BA
Tel: 01832 272349

Merry's Auctions
Northampton Auction & Sales
Centre
Liliput Road
Brackmills
NN4 7BY
Tel: 01604 769990
northamptonauctions@cwcom.net

Southams
Corn Exchange
Thrapston
NN14 4JJ
Tel: 01832 734486

Wilfords
76 Midland Road
Wellingborough
NN8 1NR
Tel: 01933 222760

NOTTINGHAMSHIRE

Bonhams
57 Mansfield Road
Nottingham
NG1 3PL
Tel: 0115 947 4414
www.bonhams.com

Arthur Johnson & Sons
The Nottingham Auction Centre
Meadow Lane
Nottingham
NG2 3GY
Tel: 0115 986 9128

Mellors & Kirk
The Auction House
Gregory Street
Nottingham
NG7 2NL
Tel: 0115 979 0000
www.mellors-kirk.co.uk

Neales Auctions
192-194 Mansfield Road
Nottingham
NG1 3HU
Tel: 0115 962 4141
www.neales.co.uk

**Phillips International
Auctioneers & Valuers**
20 The Square
Retford
DN22 6XE
Tel: 01777 708633
www.phillips-auction.com

Richard Watkinson & Partners
17 Northgate
Newark
NG24 1EX
Tel: 01636 677154

OXFORDSHIRE

Bonhams
The Coach House
66 Northfield End
Henley on Thames
RG9 2BE
Tel: 01494 413637

Dreweatt Neate Holloways
49 Parsons Street
Banbury
OX16 8PF
Tel: 01295 253 197
www.dreweatt-neate.co.uk

Mallams
Bocardo House
St Michael Street
Oxford
OX1 2DR
Tel: 01865 241352

Messengers Auction Centre
27 Sheep Street
Bicester
OX6 7JF
Tel: 01869 252901
www.thesaurus.co.uk/messengers

**Phillips International
Auctioneers & Valuers**
39 Park End Street
Oxford
OX1 1JD
Tel: 01865 723524
www.phillips-auctions.com

Simmons & Sons
32 Bell Street
Henley on Thames
RG9 2BH
Tel:01491 571111
www.simmonsandsons.com

SHROPSHIRE

Halls Fine Art
Welsh Bridge Salerooms
Shrewsbury
SY3 8LA
Tel: 01743 231212
www.halls-auctioneers.ltd.uk

McCartneys
The Ox Pasture
Overton Road
Ludlow
SY8 4AA
Tel: 01584 872251

Perry & Phillips
Auction Rooms
Old Mill Antique Centre
Mill Street
Bridgnorth
WV15 5AG
Tel: 01746 762248
www.perryandphillips.co.uk

SOMERSET

Aldridges of Bath
Newark House
26-45 Cheltenham Street
Bath
BA2 3EX
Tel: 01225 462830
www.thesaurus.co.uk/alldridgesofbath

Clevedon Salerooms
Herbert Road
Clevedon
BS21 7ND
Tel: 01275 876699
www.clevedon-salerooms.com

**Cooper & Tanner
Chartered Surveyors**
The Agricultural Centre
Standerwick
Frome
BA11 2QB
Tel: 01373 831010

Gardiner Houlgate
The Old Malthouse
Comfortable Place
Upper Bristol Road
Bath
BA1 3AJ
Tel: 01225 447933

**Greenslade Taylor Hunt
Fine Art**
Magdalene House
Church Square
Taunton
TA1 1SB
Tel: 01823 332525
www.catalogs.icollector.com/greenslade

**Lawrence Fine Art
Auctioneers Ltd**
4 Linen Yard
South Street
Crewkerne
TTA18 8AB
Tel: 01460 73041
lawrencefineart@compuserve.com

Lawrences Taunton
The Corfield Hall
Magdalene Street
Taunton
TA1 1SG
Tel: 01823 330567
www.catalogs.icollector.com/Lawrence

**The London Cigarette Card
Co. Ltd**
Sutton Rd
Somerton
TA11 6QP
Tel: 01458 273452
www.londoncigcard.co.uk

Mart Road Salerooms
Office – 13 The Parade
Minehead
TA24 5NL
Tel: 01643 702281

**Phillips International
Auctioneers & Valuers**
1 Old King Street
Bath
BA1 2JT
Tel: 01225 310609
www.phillips-auction.com

Tamlyn & Son
56 High Street
Bridgewater
TA6 3BN
Tel: 01278 458241

Wellington Salerooms
Mantle Street
Wellington
TA21 8AR
Tel: 01823 664815

Wells Auction Rooms
66-68 Southover
Wells
BA5 1UH
Tel: 01749 678094

STAFFORDSHIRE

Bagshaws
The Estate Saleroom
High Street
Uttoxeter
ST14 7HP
Tel: 01889 562811

H. Chesters & Son
196 Waterloo Road
Burslem
Stoke on Trent
ST6 3HQ
Tel: 01782 822344

John German
1 Lichfield Street
Burton on Trent
DE14 3QZ
Tel: 01283 512244

Hall & Lloyd Auctioneers
South Street
Stafford
ST16 2DZ
Tel: 01785 258176

**Louis Taylor Fine Art
Auctioneers**
Britannia House
10 Town Road
Hanley
Stoke on Trent
ST1 2QG
Tel: 01782 214111

Wintertons
Lichfield Auction Centre
Fradley Park
Fradley
Lichfield
WS13 8NF
Tel: 01543 263256

SUFFOLK

Abbotts Auction Rooms
Campsea Ash
Woodbridge
IP13 OPS
Tel: 01728 746323

**Boardman Fine Art
Auctioneers**
Station Road Corner
Haverhill
CB9 OEY
Tel: 01440 730414

Bungay Auction Rooms
7 Trinity Street
Bungay
NR35 1EH
Tel: 01986 896666

**Diamond Mills & Co. Fine Art
Auctioneers**
117 Hamilton Road
Felixstowe
P11 7BL
Tel: 01394 282281
diamondmills@easynet.com

Durrant's Auction Rooms
10 New Market
Beccles
NR34 9HA
Tel: 01502 713490
durrants.auctionrooms
@virginnet.co.uk

Dyson & Son
The Auction Room
Church Street
Clare
CO10 8PD
Tel: 01787 277993

Lacy Scott & Knight Fine Art & Furniture
10 Risbygate Street
Bury St Edmunds
IP33 3AA
Tel: 01284 755991
www.thesaurus.co.uk/lacy-scott
@knight/

Neal Sons & Fletcher
26 Church Street
Woodbridge
IP12 1DP
Tel: 01394 382263
www.nsf.co.uk

Olivers
The Saleroom
Burkitts Lane
Sudbury
CO10 1HB
Tel: 01787 880305

Phillips International Auctioneers & Valuers – East Anglia
32 Boss Hall Road
Ipswich
IP1 5DJ
Tel: 01473 740494
www.phillips-auction.com

SURREY

Clarke Gammon Fine Art Auctioneers & Valuers
The Guildford Auction Rooms
Bedford Road
Guildford
GU1 4SJ
Tel: 01483 880915

Croydon Auction Rooms
145-151 London Road
Croydon
CRO 2RG
Tel: 020 8688 1123

Ewbank Fine Art Auctioneers
Burnt Common Auction Rooms
London Road
Send
Woking
GU23 7LN
Tel: 01483 223101
www.ewbank.demon.co.uk

Hamptons International Auctioneers & Valuers
Queen Street Salerooms
Queen Street
Godalming
GU7 1BA
Tel: 01483 423497
www.hamptons-int.com

Hamptons International Auctioneers & Valuers
Baverstock House
93 High Street
Godalming
GU7 1AL
Tel: 01483 423567
www.hamptons.co.uk

Lawrences' Auctioneers Ltd
Norfolk House
80 High Street
Bletchingley
RH1 4PA
Tel: 01883 743323

Parkins
18 Malden Road
Cheam
SM3 8SD
Tel: 020 8644 6633/4
www.urus.globalnet.co.uk/~parkins

Richmond & Surrey Auctions
The Old Railway Parcels Depot
Richmond Station
Kew Road
Richmond
TW9 2NA
Tel: 020 8948 6677/6774

P. F. Windibank Fine Art Auctioneers & Valuers
Dorking Halls
Reigate Road
Dorking
RH4 1SG
Tel: 01306 884556/876280
www.windibank.co.uk

Sussex East

Bonhams
19 Palmeira Square
Hove
Brighton
BN3 2JN
Tel: 01273 220000
www.bonhams.co.uk

Burstow & Hewett
Abbey Auction Galleries and
Granary Salerooms
Battle
TN33 OAT
Tel: 01424 772374

Gorringe's Auction Galleries
Terminus Road
Bexhill on Sea
TN39 3LR
Tel: 01424 224035/212994
www.gorringes.co.uk

Gorringe's Auction Galleries
15 North Street
Lewes
BN7 2PD
Tel: 01273 472503
www.gorringes.co.uk

Graves, Son & Pilcher Fine Arts
Hove Auction Rooms
Hove Street
Hove
BN3 2GL
Tel: 01273 735266
gspfa@pavilion.co.uk

Edgar Horn's Fine Art Auctioneers
46-50 South Street
Eastbourne
BN21 4XB
Tel: 01323 410419
www.thesaurus.co.uk/edgarhorn

Raymond P. Inman
The Auction Galleries
35 & 40 Temple Street
Brighton
BN1 3BH
Tel: 01273 774777

Lewes Auction Rooms
56 High Street
Lewes
BN7 1XE
Tel: 01273 478221
www.lewesauctions.com

Wallis & Wallis
West Street Auction Galleries
Lewes
BN7 2NJ
Tel: 01273 480208
www.wallisandwallis.co.uk

Sussex West

John Bellman Ltd
New Pound
Wisborough Green
Billingshurst
RH14 OAZ
Tel: 01403 700858

Denham's
The Auction Galleries
Warnham
Nr Horsham
RH12 3RZ
Tel: 01403 255699

R. H. Ellis & Sons Auctioneers & Valuers
44-46 High Street
Worthing
BN11 1LL
Tel: 01903 288999

King & Chasemore
Midhurst Auction Rooms
West Street
Midhurst
GU29 9NQ
Tel: 01730 812456

Phillips Fine Art Salerooms
Baffins Hall
Baffins Lane
Chichester
PO19 1UA
Tel: 01243 787548
www.phillips-auction.com

Sotheby's Sussex
Summers Place
Billingshurst
RH14 9AD
Tel: 01403 833500
www.sothebys.com

Stride & Son
Southdown House
St John's Street
Chichester
PO19 1XQ
Tel: 01243 780207
stride-auction@cyberquest.co.uk

Worthing Auction Galleries Ltd
Fleet House
Teville Gate
Worthing
BN11 1UA
Tel: 01903 205565
www.worthing-auctions.co.uk

TYNE AND WEAR

Anderson & Garland
Fine Art Salerooms
Marlborough House
Marlborough Crescent
Newcastle upon Tyne
NE1 4EE
Tel: 0191 232 6278
www.auction-net.co.uk

Anderson & Garland
Kepier Chare
Crawcrook
Ryton
NE40 4TS
Tel: 0191 413 8348

Boldon Auction Galleries
24a Front Street
East Boldon
NE36 OSJ
Tel: 0191 537 2630

Corbitt's
5 Mosley Street
Newcastle upon Tyne
NE1 1YE
Tel: 0191 2327268
www.corbitts.com

Thomas N. Miller Auctioneers
Algernon Road
Byker
Newcastle upon Tyne
NE6 2UN
Tel: 0191 265 8080
millerlot@aol.com

WARWICKSHIRE

BBG Locke & England
18 Guy Street
Leamington Spa
CV32 4RT
Tel: 01926 889100
www.catalogs.icollector.com/locke

Bigwood Auctioneers Ltd
The Old School
Tiddington
Stratford upon Avon
CV37 7AW
Tel: 01789 269415
www.bigwoodauctioneers.co.uk

Henley-in-Arden Auction Sales Ltd
The Estate Office
Warwick Rd
Henley-in-Arden
B95 5BH
Tel: 01564 792154

Phillips Brothers
The Sale Room
Bearley Road
Snitterfield
Stratford upon Avon
Tel: 01789 731114

Shortland Horne Ltd
Warwick Gate
21-22 Warwick Row
Coventry
CV1 1ET
Tel: 01827 718912

Warwick & Warwick Ltd
Chalon House
Scar Bank
Millers Road
Warwick
CV34 5DB
Tel: 01926 499031

West Midlands

Biddle & Webb
Icknield Square
Ladywood
Middleway
Birmingham
B16 OPP
Tel: 0121 455 8042
antiques@biddleandweb.freeserve.co.uk

Fellows & Sons
Augusta House
19 Augusta Street
Hockley
Birmingham
B18 6JA
Tel: 0121 212 2131
www.fellows.co.uk

Old Hill Antiques & Auction Rooms
220 Halesowen Road
Old Hill
Cradley Heath
B64 6HN
Tel: 01384 411121

Phillips International Auctioneers & Valuers – Midlands
The Old House
Station Road
Knowle
Solihull
B93 OHT
Tel: 01564 776151
www.phillips-auction.com

Walker Barnett & Hill
Waterloo Rd Salerooms
Clarence Street
Wolverhampton
WV1 4JE
Tel: 01902 773531
www.thesarus.co.uk/wbh

Weller & Dufty Ltd
141 Bromsgrove Street
Birmingham
B5 6RQ
Tel: 0121 692 1212/414
www.welleranddufty.co.uk

WILTSHIRE

Hamptons Auctioneers & Valuers
20 High Street
Marlborough
SN8 1AA
Tel: 01672 516161

Laynes House Auctions
Laynes House
Oaksey
SN16 9SE
Tel: 01666 577603
lyon@lyon-oliver.demon.co.uk

Swindon Auction Rooms
The Planks
Old Town
Swindon
SN3 1QP
Tel: 01793 615915

Woolley & Wallis
Salisbury Salerooms Ltd
51-61 Castle Street
Salisbury
SP1 3SU
Tel: 01722 424500
www.auctions-on-line.com/WoolleyWallis

WORCESTERSHIRE

Griffiths & Co.
57 Foregate Street
Worcester
WR1 1DZ
Tel: 01905 26464

Philip Laney
Malvern Auction Centre
Portland Road
Off Victoria Road
Malvern
WR14 2TA
Tel: 01684 893933

Phipps & Pritchard
Bank Buildings
Exchange Street
Kidderminster
DY10 1BU
Tel: 01562 822244

Philip Serrell Auctioneers & Valuers
The Malvern Saleroom
Barnard Green Road
Malvern
WR14 3LW
Tel: 01684 892314
serrell.auctions@virgin.net

YORKSHIRE EAST

Gilbert Baitson
The Edwardian Auction Galleries
Wiltshire Road
Hull
HU4 6PG
Tel: 01482 500500
www.gilbert-baitson.co.uk

Clegg & Son
68 Aire Street
Goole
DN14 5QE
Tel: 01405 763140
www.cleggandson.co.uk

Dee, Atkinson & Harrison
The Exchange Saleroom
Driffield
YO25 7LJ
Tel: 01377 253151
www.dee.atkinson.harrison.co.uk

H. Evans & Sons Auctioneers & Valuers
1 Parliament Street
Hull
HU1 2AR
Tel: 01482 323033

Spencers Auctioneers & Estate Agents
The Imperial and Repository Salerooms
18 Quay Road
Bridlingrton
YO15 2AP
Tel: 01262 676724

YORKSHIRE NORTH

Bairstow Eves Fine Art
West End Rooms
The Paddock
Whitby
YO21 3AX
Tel: 01947 820033/820011

Bonhams
Market Chambers
14 Market Street
Bedale
DL8 1EQ
Tel: 01677 424114
www.bonhams.com

Boulton & Cooper Ltd
St Michaels House
Market Place
Malton
YO17 OLR
Tel: 01653 696151

Hutchinson-Scott
The Grange
Marton-le-Moor
Ripon
HG4 5AT
Tel: 01423 324264

Morphets of Harrogate
6 Albert Street
Harrogate
HG1 1JL
Tel: 01423 530030
www.morphets.co.uk

Scarthingwell Auction Centre
Scarthingwell
Tadcaster
LS24 9PG
Tel: 01937 557955

Stephensons
10 Colliergate
York
YO1 8BP
Tel: 01904 625533

Summersgill Auctioneers
8 Front Street
Acomb
York
YO24 3BZ
Tel: 01904 791131

Tennants Auctioneers
The Auction Centre
Harmby Road
Leyburn
DL8 5SG
Tel: 01969 623780
www.tennants.co.uk

YORKSHIRE SOUTH

A. E. Dowse & Son
Cornwall Galleries
Scotland Street
Sheffield
S3 7DE
Tel: 0114 2725858

YORKSHIRE WEST

De Rome
12 New John Street
Westgate
Bradford
BD1 2QY
Tel: 01274 734116

Andrew Hartley Fine Arts
Victoria Hall Salerooms
Little Lane
Ilkley
LS29 8EA
Tel: 01943 816363

**Phillips International
Auctioneers & Valuers**
Hepper House
17a East Parade
Leeds
LS1 2BH
Tel: 0113 2448011
www.phillips.auction.com
John H. Raby & Son
Salem Auction Rooms
21 St Mary's Road
Bradford
BD8 7QL
Tel: 01274 491121

CHANNEL ISLANDS

**Bonhams & Langlois
Auctioneers**
Westaway Chambers
Don Street
St Helier
Jersey
JE2 4TR
Tel: 01534 722441
www.bonhams.com

Bonhams Martel Maides
Allez Street Auction Rooms
St Peter Port
Guernsey
GY1 1NG
Tel: 01481 722 700

SCOTLAND

Bonhams Scotland
24 Melville Street
Edinburgh
Midlothian
EH3 7NS
Tel: 0131 226 3204
www.bonhams.com

Frasers Auctioneers
8a Harbour Road
Inverness
1V1 1SY
Tel: 01463 232395

Leslie & Leslie
Haddington
East Lothian
EH41 3JJ
Tel: 01620 822241
Loves Auction Rooms
52-54 Canal Street
Perth
Perthshire
PH2 8LF
Tel: 01738 633337

**Macdougalls Auctioneers &
Valuers**
Lower Breakish
Breakish
Isle of Skye
1V42 8QA
Tel:01471 822777

McTear's
Clydeway Business Centre
8 Elliot Place
Glasgow
G3 8EP
Tel: 0141 221 4456
www.mctears.co.uk

John Milne
9 North Silver Street
Aberdeen
Aberdeenshire
AB1 1RJ
Tel: 01224 639336
info@john-milnedemon.co.uk

**Paterson's Auctioneers &
Valuers**
8 Orchard Street
Paisley
Glasgow
PA1 1UZ
Tel: 0141 889 2435

**Phillips International
Auctioneers & Valuers –
Scotland**
65 George Street
Edinburgh
EH2 2JL
Tel: 0131 225 2266
www.phillips-auction.com

L .S. Smellie & Sons Ltd
The Furniture Market
Lower Auchingramont Road
Hamilton
Lanarkshire
ML3 6HW
Tel: 01698 282007

Taylor's Auction Rooms
11 Panmure Row
Montrose
Angus
DD10 8HH
Tel: 01674 672775

**Thomson, Roddick & Laurie
Ltd**
20 Murray Street
Annan
Dumfriesshire
DG12 6EG
Tel: 01461 202575

**Thomson, Roddick & Medcalf
Ltd**
60 Whitesands
Dumfries
Dumfriesshire
DG1 2RS
Tel: 01387 255366
office.trm@virgin.net

**Thomson, Roddick & Medcalf
Ltd**
44/3 Hardengreen Business Park
Eskbank
Edinburgh
Midlothian
EH22 3NX
Tel: 0131 454 9090

WALES

Dodds Property World
Victoria Auction Galleries
Mold
Flintshire
CH7 1EB
Tel: 01352 755705

Peter Francis
Curiosity Salerooms
19 King Street
Carmarthen
South Wales
SA31 1BH
Tel: 01267 233456/7
www.peter.francis.co.uk

Harry Ray & Co.
Lloyds Bank Chambers
Broad Street
Welshpool
SY21 7RR
Tel: 01938 552555

Rennies
87 Monnow Street
Monmouth
Gwent
NP5 3EW
Tel: 01600 712916

Welsh Country Auctions
2 Carmarthen Road
Cross Hands
Llanelli
SA14 6JP
Tel: 01269 844428

FAIRS AND MARKETS

This list of fairs and markets is
grouped alphabetically by the name
of the event organiser and
information about frequency is given
after each entry (the events vary in
size and the number of stalls is given
where predictable). You will need to
contact the organiser to confirm the
exact dates of the fairs as only a loose
guide is given – you may also
discover other events that they have
organised in your area.
Alternatively, check your facts at
www.antiquesworld.co.uk where
they have a complete Antiques Diary.

Happy hunting!

LONDON

The Brocante Fair
Olympia Exhibition Centre
Hammersmith Road
Hammersmith
W14
Adams Antiques Fairs:
020 7254 4054
*Three times a year (February, April
and September) – 200 stalls*
www.adams-antiques-fairs.co.uk

Antiques & Collectors' Fair
The Royal Horticultural Hall
Greycoat Street
Victoria
SW1
Adams Antiques Fairs:
020 7254 4054
Monthly – over 200 stalls
www.adams-antiques-fairs.co.uk

Antiques Fair
The Chelsea Town Hall
King's Road
Chelsea
SW3
Adams Antiques Fairs:
020 7254 4054
Monthly – over 70 stalls
www.adams-antiques-fairs.co.uk

Alfie's Antiques Market
13-25 Church Street
Marylebone
NW8
Contact: 020 7723 6066
*Weekly (every Tues to Sat) – general
antiques*

The London Arms Fair
The Royal National Hotel
Bedford Way
WC1
Arms Fair Ltd: 020 8539 5278
Bi-annually (April and September)

The BADA (British Antique Dealers' Association) Antiques & Fine Art Fair
The Duke of York's Headquarters
Kings Road
Chelsea
SW3
Contact: 020 7589 6108
*Annually (end of March) – 100
stalls*
www.bada-antiques-fair.co.uk

Antique Map & Print Fair
The Bonnington Hotel
Southampton Row
WC1
Contact: 01242 514287
*Monthly (usually second Monday of
the month)
The only monthly antique map and
print fair in the world!*

Charing Cross Markets
1 Embankment Place
The Embankment
WC10
Contact: 01483 281771
*Weekly (Saturdays) – stamps, coins,
postcards*

**The Commonwealth Institute
Coin Fair**
The Commonwealth Institute
Kensington High Street
W8
Contact: 020 8656 4583
*Monthly – wide range of coins
(English and foreign)*

**The LAPADA (The London
& Provincial Antique Dealers'
Association) Fair**
The Commonwealth Institute
Kensington High Street
Kensington
W8
Centre Exhibitions:
0121 767 2665
*Bi-annually (January and October)
– 105 stalls*
www.lapadafair.co.uk

The Great Antiques Fair
Earls Court Exhibition Centre
Earls Court
SW5
Clarion Events Ltd:
020 7370 8188
Annually (October) – 200 stalls

**The Spring Olympia Fine Art
& Antiques Fair**
Olympia Exhibition Centre
Hammersmith Rd
Hammersmith
W14
Clarion Events Ltd:
020 7370 8188
*Annually (end of February) – 200
stalls*

**The Summer Olympia Fine
Art & Antiques Fair**
Olympia Exhibition Centre
Hammersmith Road
Hammersmith
W14
Clarion Events Ltd:
020 7370 8188
Annually (mid-June) – 400 stalls

**The Winter Olympia Fine Art
& Antiques Fair**
The National Hall
Olympia Exhibition Centre
Hammersmith Road
Hammersmith
W14
Clarion Events Ltd:
020 7370 8188
Annually (November) – 200 stalls

**The International Antique
Scientific & Medical
Instrument Fair**
The Radisson SAS Portman Hotel
Portman Square
W1
Contact: 020 8866 8659
Annually (October)

Antiques & Collectors' Fair
The Lee Valley Leisure Centre
Picketts Lock Lane (Off Meridan
Way)
Edmonton
N9
DMG Fairs: 01636 702326
Monthly – 400 stalls

**The Wembley Antiques
& Collectors' Fair**
Hall 3
The Wembley Exhibition Centre
Empire Way
Wembley
DMG Fairs: 01636 702326
*Bi-annually (July and October) –
500 stalls*

The Ephemera Society Fair
The Hotel Russell
Russell Square
WC1
The Ephemera Society:
01923 829079
*Bi-annually (June and December)
– 50-60 stalls*

The Ephemera Society Bazaar
The Bonnington Hotel
92 Southampton Row
WC1
The Ephemera Society:
01923 829079
Seven times a year – 25 stalls

**The London International
Antique & Artist Dolls, Toys,
Miniatures & Teddy Bear Fair**
Kensington Town Hall
Exhibition & Conference Facility
Hornton Street
W8
Grannies' Goodies: 020 8693 5432
*Five times a year (February, April,
June, September and November) –
300 stalls
The biggest toy and doll fair in
Europe*

Grays Antiques Market
1-7 Davies Mews
W1
Contact: 020 7629 7034
*Weekly (Monday to Friday) – over
300 dealers*

**The Decorative Antiques
& Textiles Fair**
The Marquee
Riverside Terrace
Battersea Park
SW11
Heritage Fairs: 020 7624 5173
*Three times a year (January, April
and September) – 130 stalls*
www.decorativefair.co.uk

Antiques Fair
The Rembrandt Hotel
Thurloe Place
SW7
Heritage Antiques Fairs:
020 7624 5173
Monthly – 60 stalls

Antiques Fair
Hotel Inter-continental London
1 Hamilton Place
Hyde Park Corner
W1
Heritage Antiques Fairs:
020 7624 5173
*Bi-annually (January and
September) – 80 stalls*

Antiques Fair
The London Marriott Hotel
Grosvenor Square
W1
Heritage Antiques Fairs:
020 7624 5173
*Five times a year (January, April,
July, November and December)*

Antiques Fair
The Lanesborough
1 Lanesborough Place
SW1
Heritage Antiques Fairs:
020 7624 5173
Seven times a year

Antiques & Collectors' Fair
St Mark's Church Hall
Compton Road
Wimbledon
SW19
P & J Hobbs: 020 8542 4675
*Monthly (usually last Saturday of
the month)*

Antiques & Collectors' Fair
The St Andrews Hall
Chase Side
Southgate
N14
M & S Enterprises:
020 8440 2330
Monthly – 70 stalls

Antiques & Collectors' Fair
Muswell Hill Centre
Muswell Hill Road
N10
M & S Enterprises:
020 8440 2330
Monthly – 40 stalls

Antiques & Collectors' Fair
St Andrews School
Totteridge Lane
N20
M & S Enterprises:
020 8440 2330
Monthly – 40 stalls

Antiques Fair
The Chelsea Town Hall
King's Road
SW3
Mainwarings Antiques Fairs:
01225 723094
Monthly – 80 stalls

Antiques Fair
St Paul's Church Hall
The Ridgeway
NW7
Marcel Fairs: 020 8950 1844
*Monthly (usually first Saturday of
the month) – 30 stalls*

Antiques Fair
The Atkinson Morley's Hall
Copse Hill
Wimbledon
SW20
P & A Antiques: 020 8543 5075
Monthly – 35 stalls

The Decorative Arts Fair
Fulham Town Hall
Fulham Broadway
SW6
P & A Antiques: 020 8543 5075
Annually (July) – 55-70 stalls

**The Kensington Antiques
& Fine Art Fair**
Kensington Town Hall
Hornton Street
W8
Penman Fairs: 01444 482514
*Bi-annually (January and August)
– 50 stalls of antiques and 20 stalls
of contemporary art*
www.penman-fairs.co.uk

The Chelsea Antiques Fair
Chelsea Old Town Hall
King's Road
Chelsea
SW3
Penman Fairs: 01444 482514
*Bi-annually (March and
September) – 40 stalls*
www.penman-fairs.co.uk

The Chelsea Art Fair
Chelsea Old Town Hall
King's Road
SW3
Penman Fairs: 01444 482514
*Annually (April) – 48 artists and
galleries exhibit*
www.penman-fairs.co.uk

**The Alexandra Palace
Antiques & Collectors' Fair**
The Great Hall
Alexandra Palace
Wood Green
N22
Pig & Whistle Promotions:
020 8883 7061
Five times a year – 700 stalls

Antiques Market
Portobello Road
Notting Hill
W11
*Weekly (Fridays and Saturdays) –
over 300 stalls and shops*

The London Coin Fair
The Cumberland Hotel
Carlisle Suite
Marble Arch
W1
Frances Simmons: 020 7831 2080
*Four times a year (February, June,
September and November)
The biggest coin fair in Britain*

The London Paper Money Fair
The Bonnington Hotel
92 Southampton Row
WC1
West Promotions: 020 8641 3224
Monthly

**The Grosvenor House Art
& Antiques Fair**
Grosvenor House
Park Lane
London
W1
Contact: 020 7589 4128
Annually (mid-June) – 90 stalls

HOME COUNTIES

Antiques Fair
The Big Venue
Luton Sports Centre
Luton
Hertfordshire
A1 Fairs: 01702 203503
*Annually (February) – over 200
stalls*

Antiques & Collectors' Market
The Goodwood Racecourse
Near Chichester
West Sussex
Antiques & Collectors World:
01737 812989
*Three times a year (March, July
and August) – 500 stalls*

Collectors' Fair
The Lockswood Community
Centre
Locks Heath
Near Fareham
Hampshire
Athena Fayres: 01489 584633
Monthly – 30-40 stalls

Antiques & Collectors' Fair
The Village Hall
Minstead
New Forest
Hampshire
Athena Fayres: 01489 584633
Monthly – 25-30 stalls

Antiques & Collectors' Fair
The Community Centre
Mill Lane
Wickham
Hampshire
Athena Fayres: 01489 584633
Monthly – 70-80 stalls

Antiques & Collectors' Fair
The Beasconsfield Masonic
Centre
Windsor End
Old Beasconsfield
Buckinghamshire
BC Antiques Fairs:
020 8950 1844
Monthly

**The Hertfordshire Antiques
& Fine Art Fair**
Hatfield House
The Goscoyne Cecil Estate
Hatfield Park
Hertfordshire
Bailey Fairs: 01277 214699
Annually (November)

The Luton Antiques Fair
The Putteridge Bury House
Luton
Hertfordshire
Contact: 01234 381701
*Bi-annually (February and
October) – 42 stalls*

The Mid-Beds Antiques Fair
Silsoe College and Conference
Centre
Silsoe
Bedfordshire
Contact: 01234 381701
*Bi-annually (March and
November) – 40 stalls*

Antiques & Collectors' Fair
The Tolworth Recreation Centre
A3 Kingston Bypass
Surrey
Big Surrey Fairs Ltd:
020 8390 1230
Annually (March)

Antiques & Collectors' Fair
The Leisure Centre
Hurst Road
Walton-on-Thames
Surrey
Big Surrey Fairs Ltd:
020 8390 1230
Bi-annually (July and September)

Antiques & Collectors' Fair
The Canons Leisure Centre
Madeira Road
Mitcham
Surrey
Big Surrey Fairs Ltd:
020 8390 1230
Annually (March)

Antiques Fair
The Castle Hall
Hertford
Hertfordshire
Camfair Antiques: 01945 870160
Monthly

Antiques & Collectables Fair
The St Crispin's Sports Centre
London Road
Berkshire
Crispins Fairs: 0118 983 3020
Monthly

Antiques & Collectors' Fair
The Victoria Hall
Hartley Wintney
Hampshire
Crispins Fairs: 0118 983 3020
Monthly

Antiques & Collectors' Fair
The Copthorne Effingham Park
Hotel
West Park Road
Copthorne
West Sussex
Cross Country Fairs Ltd:
01474 834120
Monthly

The Surrey Antiques Fair
Civic Hall
Guildford
Surrey
Cultural Exhibitions Ltd:
01483 422562
Annually (October)

Antiques & Collectors' Fair
The Ditchling Village Hall
Lewes Road
Ditchling
Sussex
Contact: 01273 845141
Bi-monthly

**The Ardingly International
Antiques & Collectors' Fair**
The South of England
Showground
Ardingly
Sussex
DMG Antiques Fairs:
01636 702326
Monthly – 2000 stalls

Antiques & Collectors' Fair
The County Showground
Detling
Maidstone
Kent
DMG Antiques Fairs:
01636 702326
Monthly – 40 shopping arcades

**The Malvern Antiques
& Collectors' Fair**
Three Counties Showground
Malvern
Worcestershire
DMG Antiques Fairs:
01636 702326
Monthly – 250 stalls

Toy & Train Fair
The Elm Court Youth &
Community Centre
Mutton Lane
Potters Bar
Hertfordshire
DPL Fairs: 020 8205 1518
*Bi-annually (September and
November)*

Camera Fair
St Peter's Catholic School
Horseshoe Lane East
Merrow
Guildford
Surrey
DPL Fairs: 020 8205 1518
Anually (October)

Toy & Train Fair
The Edgware School
Green Lane
Off Spur Road
Edgware
Middlesex
DPL Fairs: 020 8205 1518
*Bi-annually (October and
December)*

Toy & Train Fair
The John Bunyan Upper School
Mile Road
Bedford
Bedfordshire
DPL Fairs: 020 8205 1518
*Three times a year (July, October
and November)*

Camera Fair
The Francis Bacon School
Drakes Drive
St Albans
Hertfordshire
DPL Fairs: 020 8205 1518
Annually (July)

Camera Fair
The Shaw House School
Church Road/Love Lane
Newbury
Buckinghamshire
DPL Fairs: 020 8205 1518
Annually (August)

**Toy & Train Fair
and Camera Fair**
The Beaconsfield School
Wattleton Road
Beaconsfield
Buckinghamshire
DPL Fairs: 020 8205 1518
*Bi-annually (September and
November)*

Camera Fair
The Allum Hall
Allum Lane
Elstree
Hertfordshire
DPL Fairs: 020 8205 1518
Annually (November)

**The Brunel Clock
& Watch Fair**
Brunel University
Kingston Lane
Uxbridge
Middlesex
Contact: 01895 834694
*Bi-annually (September and
December)*

Antiques Fair
The Cresset
Bretton centre
Peterborough
Bob Evans Fairs: 01733 265705
Annually (February) – 200 stalls

Antiques & Collectors' Fair
The Community Centre
Buckingham
E. W. Services Antiques Fairs:
01933 225674
Monthly

Antiques & Collectors' Fair
The Community Centre
Baldock
Hertfordshire
E. W. Services Antiques Fairs:
01933 225674
Monthly

**The Milton Keynes
Antiques Fair**
The Middleton Hall
Central Milton Keynes
Regional Shopping Centre
Buckinghamshire
E. W. Services Antiques Fairs:
01933 225674
*Bi-annually (February and
September)*

Antiques Fair
St Michaels' Catholic High
School
North Watford
Hertfordshire
E. W. Services Antiques Fairs:
01933 225674
Monthly

Antiques Fair
Hatfield Galleria Retail Outlet
Centre
Comet Way
Hatfield
Hertfordshire
E. W. Services Antiques Fairs:
01933 225674
*Bi-annually (September and
November)*

Antiques Fair
Seaford College
Near Petworth
West Sussex
Galloway Antiques Fairs:
01423 522122
Annually (October)

Antiques Fair
Cranleigh School
Cranleigh
Surrey
Galloway Antiques Fairs:
01423 522122
Annually (July)

Antiques & Collectors' Fair
The Masonic Hall
Lymington
Hampshire
Grandma's Attic Fairs:
01590 677687
Monthly – 32 stalls

Antiques & Collectors' Fair
The Brockenhurst Village Hall
Highwood Road
New Forest
Brockenhurst
Hampshire
Grandma's Attic Fairs:
01590 677687
Monthly – 45 stalls

Antiques & Collectors' Fair
The Lyndhurst Park Hotel
High Street
Lyndhurst
Hampshire
Grandma's Attic Fairs:
01590 677687
Monthly

Antiques & Collectors' Fair
The Winchester Guildhall
The Broadway
Winchester
Hampshire
Grandma's Attic Fairs:
01590 677687
Monthly – 70 stalls

Antiques & Collectors' Fair
St Thomas' Church Hall
Lymington
Hampshire
Grandma's Attic Fairs:
01590 677687
Bi-annually (September and November)

Antiques & Collectors' Fair
The Potters Heron Hotel
Hampshire
Grandma's Attic Fairs:
01590 677687
Bi-annually (October and December)

Antiques & Collectors' Fair
Botleigh Grange
Botley Hedge End
Hampshire
Grandma's Attic Fairs:
01590 677687
Annually (October)

Antiques Fair
The Centre for Epilepsy
Chalfont St Peter
Buckinghamshire
Harlequin Fairs: 01462 671688
Monthly

Antiques Fair
The Elstree Moat House Hotel
Hertfordshire
Harlequin Fairs: 01462 671688
Monthly

Antiques Fair
The Lister Harpur Suite
Corn Exchange Complex
Bedford
Bedfordshire
Janba Fairs: 01945 870160
Bi-annually (October and December)

Antiques Market
The Town Hall
Hungerford
Berkshire
Jay Fairs: 01235 815633
Monthly

Antiques & Collectors' Fair
The Shiplake Memorial Hall
Shiplake
Near Henley on Thames
Oxfordshire
Jay Fairs: 01235 815633
Monthly – 20 stalls

Antiques & Collectors' Fair
Crowmarsh Village Hall
Near Wallingford
Oxfordshire
Jay Fairs: 01235 815633
Annually (August) – 20 stalls

Antiques & Collectors' Fair
Drayton Village Hall
Near Abingdon
Oxfordshire
Jay Fairs: 01235 815633
Bi-annually (September and November) – 20 stalls

Antiques & Collectors' Fair
The Village Hall
Dorchester on Thames
Oxfordshire
Jay Fairs: 01235 815633
Bi-annually (October and December)

Flea Market
The Civic Hall
Didcot
Oxfordshire
Jay Fairs: 01235 815633
Bi-annually (October and December)

Antiques & Collectors' Fair
The Royal Chace Hotel
Queens Banqueting Suite
The Ridgeway
Enfield
Middlesex
M & S Enterprises:
020 8440 2330
Three times a year (September, October and November)

Antiques Fair
The Grange Centre
Bepton Road
Midhurst
West Sussex
Magnum Antiques Fairs:
01491 681009
Bi-monthly – 130 stalls

Antiques Fair
The River Park Leisure Centre
Gordon Road
Winchester
Hampshire
Magnum Antiques Fairs:
01491 681009
Bi-annually (August and October) – 170 stalls

Antiques Fair
The Bellhouse Hotel
Oxford Road
Beaconsfield
Buckinghamshire
Midas Fairs: 01494 674170
Monthly

Fine Art & Antiques Fair
The Bellhouse Hotel
Oxford Road
Beaconsfield
Buckinghamshire
Midas Fairs: 01494 674170
Annually (August)

Antiques & Collectors' Fair
The Victoria Hall
Hartley Wintney
Hampshire
Midweek Fairs: 0118 950 2960
Monthly

Antiques Fair
The Brighton Centre
Kings Road
Brighton
Sussex
Shirley Mostyn Fairs:
01903 752961
*Bi-annually (August and
December)*

Antiques Fair
The Hove Town Hall
Norton Road
Hove
Sussex
Shirley Mostyn Fairs:
01903 752961
Monthly

The Petersfield Antiques Fair
The Festival Hall
Petersfield
Hampshire
Penman Fairs: 01444 482514
*Three times a year (February, June
and September)*

Antiques & Collectors' Fair
The Hickstead Showground
London Road
Hickstead
West Sussex
R&S Fairs: 01702 345222
Annually (September)

Antiques & Collectors' Fair
The Dolphin Leisure Centre
Pasture Hill Road
Haywards Heath
West Sussex
R&S Fairs: 01702 345222
Annually (October)

Antiques Fair
The Bashley Village Hall
Bashley
Hampshire
Renaissance Fairs: 01202 319914
Monthly

Antiques & Collectors' Fair
The Royal Enclosure
The Racecourse
Ascot
Berkshire
Silhouette Fairs: 01635 44338
Monthly

Antiques & Collectors' Fair
The Abbey Hall
Abingdon
Oxfordshire
Silhouette Fairs: 01635 44338
Monthly

South East Antiques Fairs
Donnington Manor Hotel
London Road
Dunton Green
Sevenoaks
Kent
South East Fairs: 01892 653379
*Three times a year (February,
March and October) – 35 stalls*

South East Antiques Fairs
Jarvis Felbridge Hotel
London Road
East Grinstead
West Sussex
South East Fairs: 01892 653379
Five times a year – 70 stalls

South East Antiques Fairs
Winston Manor Hotel
Beacon Road
Crowborough
East Sussex
South East Fairs: 01892 653379
*Bi-annually (June and November)
– 45 stalls*

Antiques & Collectors' Fair
The Woking Leisure Centre
Kingfield Road
Woking
Surrey
Take Five Fairs: 020 8894 0218
Annually (July)

Glass Fair
The Woking Leisure Centre
Kingfield Road
Woking
Surrey
Take Five Fairs: 020 8894 0218
Annually (October)

Antiques & Collectors' Fair
The Rainbow Centre
East Street
Epsom
Surrey
Take Five Fairs: 020 8894 0218
Annually (July)

London Art Deco
& Modernist Fair
The Canons
Madeira Road
Mitcham
Surrey
Philip Thompson:
020 8663 3323
Annually (February) – over 100
stalls of 1920s-1970s original goods

Antiques Fair
The Shuttleworth Mansion
Old Warren Park
Biggleswade
Bedfordshire
Graham Turner Antiques Fairs:
01473 658224
Annually (October)

Ceramics Fair
The Burford School
Burford
Oxfordshire
Wakefield Ceramics Fairs:
01303 258635
Bi-annually (July and October)

Country Markets, Antiques
& Collectables
Chilton Garden Centre
Newbury Road
Chilton
Didcot
Oxfordshire
Contact: 01235 835125
Permanent – 35 dealers

Ceramics Fair
The Combe Bank School
Sundridge
Near Westerham
Kent
Wakefield Ceramics Fairs:
01303 258635
Annually (July)

Ceramics Fair
Hatfield House
Hatfield
Hertfordshire
Wakefield Ceramics Fairs:
01303 258635
Annually (September)

Antiques Fairs
The Sandown Exhibition Centre
Sandown Park Racecourse
Esher
Surrey
Wonder Whistle Enterprises:
020 7249 4050
Bi-annually (October and
November)

The Barn Collectors Market
& Bookshop
Church Lane
Seaford
East Sussex
Contact: 01323 890010
Permanent

EAST ANGLIA

Antiques & Collectors' Fair
The International Arena
Wood Green Animal Shelter
London Road
Godmanchester
Huntingdon
Cambridgeshire
Aztec Fairs: 01702 233123
Bi-annually (July and September)

Antiques & Collectors' Fair
The Harlow Sports Centre
Hammarskjold Road
Harlow
Essex
Aztec Fairs: 01702 233123
Three times a year (September, October and December)

Antiques & Collectors' Fair
The Brentwood Centre
Doddinghurst Road
Brentwood
Essex
Aztec Fairs: 01702 233123
Bi-annually (August and November)

Antiques & Collectors' Fair
The Norfolk Showground
New Costessey
Norfolk
Aztec Fairs: 01702 233123
Bi-annually (August and November)

Antiques & Collectors' Fair
The Riverside Leisure Centre
Victoria Road
Chelmsford
Essex
Aztec Fairs: 01702 233123
Bi-annually (September and November)

Antiques & Collectors' Fair
The Suffolk Showground
Bucklesham Road
Ipswich
Suffolk
Aztec Fairs: 01702 233123
Bi-annually (August and October)

Antiques & Collectors' Fair
The Women's Institute Hall
Frinton on Sea
Essex
Best of Fairs: 01787 280306
Bi-annually (July and November)

Antiques & Collectors' Fair
The New Village Hall
Copdock
Nr Ipswich
Suffolk
Best of Fairs: 01787 280306
Monthly

Antiques & Collectors' Fair
The Old School
Long Melford
Suffolk
Best of Fairs: 01787 280306
Monthly

Antiques & Collectors' Fair
The Church Rooms
Lavenham
Suffolk
Best of Fairs: 01787 280306
Monthly

Antiques & Collectors' Fair
The Leisure Centre
Seafront
Felixstowe
Suffolk
Best of Fairs: 01787 280306
Most months

Antiques & Collectors' Fair
The Village Hall
Ingatestone
Nr Brentwood
Essex
Best of Fairs: 01787 280306
Bi-annually (October and December)

Antiques & Collectors' Fair
The New Village Hall
Nayland
Suffolk
Best of Fairs: 01787 280306
Bi-annually (October and December)

Antiques & Collectors' Fair
Mountnessing
Nr Brentwood
Essex
Best of Fairs: 01787 280306
Bi-annually (October and November)

Antiques & Collectors' Fair
The Church Hall
Frinton on Sea
Essex
Best of Fairs: 01787 280306
Bi-annually (November and December)

Antiques & Collectors' Fair
The Town Hall
Clare
Suffolk
Best of Fairs: 01787 280306
Annually (November)

**The Annual Snape
Antiques Fair**
Snape
Suffolk
Cooper Antiques Fairs:
01249 661111
Annually (mid-July)

Antiques & Collectors' Fair
The Newmarket Racecourse
Newmarket
Suffolk
DMG Antiques Fairs:
01636 702326
Bi-annually (August and November)

Antiques & Collectors' Fair
The Essex Country Showground
Chelmsford
Essex
DMG Antiques Fairs:
01636 702326
Three times a year (July, September and October)

The Cambridge Antiques Fair
Linton Village College
Linton
Cambridgeshire
E. W. Services Antiques Fairs:
01933 225674
Three times a year (September, October and November)

**The East Anglian Art Deco
& Decorative Arts Fair**
Linton Village College
Linton
Cambridgeshire
E. W. Services Antiques Fairs:
01933 225674
Bi-annually (August and October)

Antiques Fair
The Courage Hall
Brentwood School
Middleton Hall Lane
Brentwood
Essex
Hallmark Antiques Fairs Ltd:
01702 710383
Annually (October)

Antiques Fair
The Southend Tennis & Leisure
Centre
Eastern Avenue
Southend
Essex
Hallmark Antiques Fairs Ltd:
01702 710383
Annually (September)

Antiques Fair
The Cressing Temple Barns
Witham
Essex
Hallmark Antiques Fairs Ltd:
01702 710383
Annually (September)

Antiques Fair
The Southend Cliffs Pavilion
Station Road
Westcliff on Sea
Essex
Hallmark Antiques Fairs Ltd:
01702 710383
Annually (October)

Antiques Fair
Blakeney Village Hall
Blakeney
Norfolk
Janba Fairs: 01945 870160
Monthly

Antiques Fair
Knights Hill Hotel
Kings Lynn
Norfolk
Janba Fairs: 01945 870160
Monthly

Antiques Fair
The Burgess Hall
St Ivo Recreation Centre
St Ives
Cambridgeshire
Janba Fairs: 01945 870160
*Three times a year (August, October
and November)*

Antiques & Collectors' Fair
The Community Hall
Station Road
Woodbridge
Suffolk
Kyson Fairs: 01473 735528
Monthly

**The East Anglian Antiques
Dealers' Fair**
The Langley Park School
Loddon
Norfolk
Lomax Antiques Fairs:
01603 737631
Annually (October)

**The Woolverstone Fine Art
& Antiques Fair**
Ipswich High School for Girls
Woolverstone
Nr Ipswich
Suffolk
Lomax Antiques Fairs:
01603 737631
Annually (September)

Antiques & Collectors' Fair
The Suffolk Showground
Bucklesham Road
Ipswich
Suffolk
R&S Fairs: 01702 345222
Bi-annually (August and October)

Antiques Fair
The Brentwood Centre
Doddinghurst Road
Brentwood
Essex
R&S Fairs: 01702 345222
*Bi-annually (August and
November)*

Antiques & Collectors' Fair
The Leisure World
Cowdray Avenue
Colchester
Essex
R&S Fairs: 01702 345222
Annually (September)

Antiques & Collectors' Fair
The Sir James Hawkey Hall
Broadmead Road
Woodford Green
Essex
R&S Fairs: 01702 345222
Annually (October)

Antiques & Collectors' Fair
The Sports Centre
Harrow Lodge Park
Hornchurch Road
Hornchurch
Essex
R&S Fairs: 01702 345222
Bi-annually (October and December)

The Essex Doulton, Beswick & Wade Fair
Manhattan Suite
City Limits
Collier Row Road
Nr Romford
Essex
R&S Fairs: 01702 345222
Annually (November)

The Jewellery Clock & Watch Fair
Manhattan Suite
City Limits
Collier Row Road
Nr Romford
Essex
R&S Fairs: 01702 345222
Annually (December)

Antiques Fair
The Hollywood Restaurant
Shipwrights Drive
Thundersley
Benfleet
Essex
Ridgeway Fairs: 01702 710383
Bi-annually (September and November)

Antiques Fair
The Southend Bandstand
Clifftown Parade
Southend on Sea
Essex
Ridgeway Fairs: 01702 710383
Annually (August)

Antiques Fair
The Mill Hall
Rayleigh
Essex
Ridgeway Fairs: 01702 710383
Bi-annually (August and November)

Antiques Fair
Keys Hall
Eagle Way
Great Warley
Nr Brentwood
Essex
Ridgeway Fairs: 01702 710383
Bi-annually (October and December)

Antiques Fair
The Community Centre
Elm Road
Leigh on Sea
Essex
Ridgeway Fairs: 01702 710383
Bi-annually (October and December)

Antiques Fair
The Sports & Leisure Centre
Main Road
Danbury
Essex
Ridgeway Fairs: 01702 710383
Bi-annually (July and December)

Antiques Fair
The Marks Hall Estate
Coggeshall
Essex
Ridgeway Fairs: 01702 710383
Annually (August)

Antiques Fair
The Bartlett's Farm
East Hanningfield
Essex
Ridgeway Fairs: 01702 710383
Annually (August)

Antiques Fair
The Thurrock Civic Hall
Blackshott's Lane
Grays
Essex
Ridgeway Fairs: 01702 710383
Annually (October)

Antiques Fair
The Marconi Sports & Social
Club
Beehive Lane
Great Baddow
Chelmsford
Essex
Ridgeway Fairs: 01702 710383
Annually (October)

The Furze Hill Antiques Fair
The Banqueting Centre
Margaretting
Nr Chelmsford
Essex
Graham Turner Fairs:
01473 658224
Monthly

Antiques Fair
Little Easton Manor
Nr Great Dunmow
Essex
Graham Turner Fairs:
01473 658224
Bi-annually (July and September)

Antiques Fair
The Memorial Hall
Long Melford
Suffolk
Graham Turner Fairs:
01473 658224
Monthly

**The Antiques & Collectors'
Bygones Market**
The Triangle Market Place
High Street
Lowestoft
Suffolk
Waveney District Council:
01502 523338
Monthly

MIDLANDS

**The Buxton Autumn Fine Art
& Antiques Fair**
The Pavilion Gardens
Buxton
Derbyshire
Bailey Fairs: 01277 214699
Annually (October)

**The Warwickshire Antiques
& Fine Art Fair**
Ragley Hall
Alcester
Warwickshire
Bailey Fairs: 01277 214699
Annually (October)

**The Nottinghamshire Arts
& Antiques Fair**
The Thoresby Park
Near Ollerton
Nottinghamshire
Bailey Fairs: 01277 214699
Annually (November)

Antiques Fair
The Bingley Hall County
Showground
Stafford
Staffordshire
Bowman Antiques Fairs:
07071 284 333
Monthly

**The Carltonware
Collectors' Fair**
The North Stafford Hotel
Station Road
Stoke on Trent
Staffordshire
Carltonware Collectors'
International: 01474 853630
Annually (October)

Antiques for Everyone
Hall 5
The National Exhibition Centre
Birmingham
West Midlands
Centre Exhibitions:
0121 767 2760
*Three times a year (April, August
and November)*

The LAPADA Fair
National Exhibition Centre
Birmingham
West Midlands
Centre Exhibitions:
0121 767 2665
Annually (January) – five day fair

Birmingham Antiques Fair
St Martins Market
Edgbaston
Birmingham
West Midlands
Contact: 01782 595805
*Eight times a year – over 1000
stalls*

Moreton Hall Antiques Fair
Moreton Hall
Warwickshire College of
Agriculture
Moreton Morrell
Warwickshire
Cooper Antiques Fairs:
01249 661111
Annually (November)

Antiques & Collectors' Fair
The Town Hall
Loughborough
Leicestershire
County Fairs: 0700 0432477
*Bi-annually (September and
November)*

Antiques & Collectors' Fair
The Village Hall
Newtown Linford
Leicestershire
County Fairs: 0700 0432477
*Bi-annually (September and
December)*

Antiques & Collectors' Fair
The Parklands Leisure Centre
Oadby
Leicestershire
County Fairs: 0700 0432477
Bi-annually (July and December)

Antiques & Collectors' Fair
The Community College
Desford
Leicestershire
County Fairs: 0700 0432477
*Bi-annually (August and
November)*

Antiques & Collectors' Fair
The School
Uppingham
Leicestershire
County Fairs: 0700 0432477
Annually (August)

Antiques & Collectors' Fair
The College
Countersthorpe
Leicestershire
County Fairs: 0700 0432477
Annually (September)

Antiques & Collectors' Fair
The Village Hall
Gaddesby
Leicestershire
County Fairs: 0700 0432477
Annually (September)

Antiques & Collectors' Fair
The Sketchley Grange Hotel
Hinckley
Leicestershire
County Fairs: 0700 0432477
Annually (October)

Antiques & Collectors' Fair
The Leisure Centre
Enderby
Leicestershire
County Fairs: 0700 0432477
Annually (October)

Antiques & Collectors' Fair
The Stage Hotel
Wigston Fields
Leicestershire
County Fairs: 0700 0432477
Annually (October)

Antiques & Collectors' Fair
The Leicester City Football Club
Filbert Street
Leicester
Leicestershire
County Fairs: 0700 0432477
Annually (November)

Antiques & Collectors' Fair
The Rockingham Forest Hotel
Corby
Leicestershire
County Fairs: 0700 0432477
Annually (November)

Antiques & Collectors' Fair
The Exhibition Centre
Warwick
Warwickshire
DMG Antiques Fairs:
01636 702326
Bi-annually (October and December)

Antiques & Collectors' Fair
The Newark & Nottinghamshire
Showground
Newark
Nottinghamshire
DMG Antiques Fairs:
01636 702326
Bi-monthly

Antiques & Collectors' Fair
The National Agricultural Centre
Stoneleigh
Warwickshire
DMG Antiques Fairs:
01636 702326
Annually (November)

**The Midland Clock
& Watch Fair**
The National Motorcycle
Museum
Solihull
West Midlands
Mr Dungate: 018955 834694
Bi-annually (August and November)

Antiques Fair
The Northamptonshire County
Cricket Club
The Indoor Centre
Abington Avenue
Northampton
Northamptonshire
E. W. Services Antiques Fairs:
01933 225674
Three times a year (July, October and December)

Antiques Fair
The Wrekin College
Wellington
Shropshire
Galloway Antiques Fair:
01423 522122
Annually (August)

Antiques Fair
The Haggley Hall
Stourbridge
Worcestershire
Galloway Antiques Fairs:
01423 522122
Bi-annually (September and October)

Antiques Fair
Deene Park
Corby
Northamptonshire
Galloway Antiques Fairs:
01423 522122
Annually (October)

The Glass Collectors' Fair
The National Motorcycle
Museum
Birmingham
West Midlands
Contact: 01260 271975
Annually (November)

Antiques Fair
The Town Hall
Bakewell
Derbyshire
Peak Fairs: 01629 812449
Monthly

Antiques & Collectors' Fair
The Strafford-upon-Avon Visitor
Centre
Stratford
Warwickshire
Profile Promotions:
0121 449 4246
Monthly

Antiques & Collectors' Fair
The Warwick University
Art Centre
Central Campus
Gibbet Hill Road
Coventry
West Midlands
Profile Promotions:
0121 449 4246
Annually (August)

Antiques & Collectors' Fair
The Royal Spa Centre
Newbold Terrace
Leamington Spa
Warwickshire
Profile Promotions:
0121 449 4246
Bi-annually (September and November)

Antiques & Collectors' Fair
The King Edward VI Camp Hill
Schools
Vicarge Road
Birmingham
West Midlands
Profile Promotions:
0121 449 4246
Monthly

Antiques & Collectors' Fair
The Silverstone Motor Racing
Circuit
Silverstone
Northamptonshire
R&S Fairs: 01702 345222
Annually (July)

The National Art Deco Fair
The Town Hall
Loughborough
Leicestershire
Top Hat Exhibitions:
0115 9419143
Bi-annually (July and October)

Antiques & Collectors' Fair
The Pavilion Gardens
Buxton
Derbyshire
Unicorn Fairs Ltd:
0161 773 7001
Monthly

Ceramics Fair
The Bank House Hotel
Bransford
Worcestershire
Wakefield Ceramics Fairs:
01303 258635
Annually (November)

Antiques & Collectors' Fair
The Community Centre
Kinver
Staffordshire
Waverley Fairs: 0121 550 4123
Monthly

Antiques & Collectors' Fair
The New Market Hall
Bromsgrove
Worcestershire
Waverley Fairs: 0121 550 4123
Monthly

Book Fair
Powick Village Hall
Worcestershire
Waverley Fairs: 0121 550 4123
Monthly

Book Fair
The Community Centre
Kinver
Staffordshire
Waverley Fairs: 0121 550 4123
Monthly

Book Fair
Callow End Village Hall
Worcestershire
Waverley Fairs: 0121 550 4123
Annually (October)

Antiques Fair
The Prestwood Complex
Stafford County Showground
Weston Road
Stafford
West Midlands Antiques Fairs:
01743 271444
Monthly – 280 stalls

WEST COUNTRY

**The North Cotswold
Antiques Fair**
Stanway House
Nr Winchcombe
Gloucestershire
Cooper Antiques Fairs:
01249 661111
*Annually (July) – takes place in
14th-century tithe barn*

**The South Cotswold
Antiques Fair**
Westonbirt School
Tetbury
Gloucestershire
Cooper Antiques Fairs:
01249 661111
*Three times a year (April, August
and December) – 80 stalls*

Antiques Fair
The Westpoint Exhibition Centre
Clyst St Mary
Exeter
Devon
Cooper Antiques Fairs:
01249 661111
Monthly

Antiques & Collectors' Fair
The Salisbury Leisure Centre
The Butts
Hulse Road
Salisbury
Wiltshire
Cooper Antiques Fairs:
01249 661111
Bi-annually (September and December)

The Shepton Mallet Antiques & Collectors' Fair
The Royal Bath & West
Showground
Shepton Mallet
Somerset
DMG Antiques Fairs:
01636 702326
Bi-monthly – over 600 exhibitors

Antiques Fair
The Powerham Castle
Exeter
Devon
Galloway Antiques Fairs:
01423 522122
Annually (December)

Antiques & Collectors' Fair
Kingston Maurward House
The Dorset College of Agriculture
& Horticulture
Dorchester
Dorset
Grandma's Attic Fairs:
01590 677687
Three times a year (July, September and November)

Antiques & Collectors' Fair
The Allendale Centre
Hanham Road
Wimborne
Dorset
Grandma's Attic Antiques Fairs:
01590 677687
Three times a year (August, October and December)

Antiques & Collectors' Fair
The Littledown Centre
Castle Lane
North East of Bournemouth
Dorset
Grandma's Attic Fairs:
01590 677687
Annually (November)

Antiques & Collectors' Fair
The Pavilion
Exmouth
Devon
Sheila Hyson Fairs:
01647 231 459
Monthly

Antiques & Collectors' Fair
The Holsworthy Memorial Hall
Holsworthy
Devon
Sheila Hyson Fairs:
01647 231 459
Monthly

Antiques & Collectors' Fair
The Jubilee Hall
Chagford
Devon
Sheila Hyson Fairs:
01647 231 459
Three times a year (July, October and December)

**The West Country Specialist
Glass Fair**
Newton Abbot Racecourse
Newton Abbot
Devon
Sheila Hyson Fairs:
01647 231 459
*Annually (October) – glass, Art
Deco, 50s and 60s collectibles and
specialist textiles*

Antiques & Collectors' Fair
The Winter Gardens
Sea Front
Weston Super Mare
Avon
Melba Fairs: 01934 412923
Monthly

**The Cotswold Premier
Monthly Antiques Fair**
The Cheltenham Racecourse
Cheltenham
Gloucestershire
Contact : 01934 624854
Monthly – over 110 stalls

Antiques & Collectors' Fair
The Cheltenham Racecourse
Cheltenham
Gloucestershire
Melba Fairs: 01934 412923
Annually (August)

Antiques & Collectors' Fair
Longleat
Nr Warminster
Wiltshire
R&S Fairs: 01702 345222
Annually (August)

Antiques Fair
The Corfe Castle Village Hall
Corfe
Dorset
Renaissance Fairs: 01202 319914
Monthly

**Antiques & Collectables
Market**
The Brunel Great Train Shed
Brunel's Historic Station
Temple Meads
Bristol
Avon
Talisman Fairs: 01225 872522
Monthly

Antiques & Collectors' Fair
The Torquay Sea Front
Belgrave Hotel
Torquay
Devon
Talisman Fairs: 01225 872522
Monthly

Antiques & Collectors' Fair
The St Margaret's Hall
Bradford on Avon
Wiltshire
Talisman Fairs: 01225 872522
Monthly

**Antique Brocante
& Collectors' Fair**
The Newton Abbot Racecourse
Newton Abbot
Devon
Talisman Fairs: 01225 872522
Monthly

Jazz Art Deco Fair
The Brunel Great Train Shed
Temple Meads Station
Brunel's Historic Station
Temple Meads
Briston
Avon
Talisman Fairs: 01225 872522
Annually (October)

Ceramics Fair
The Michael Herbert Hall
Wilton
Nr Salisbury
Wiltshire
Wakefield Ceramics Fairs:
01303 258635
Annually (October)

NORTHERN COUNTIES

Antiques Fair
The Old Swan Hotel
Harrogate
North Yorkshire
Abbey Antiques Fairs:
01482 445785
Monthly – around 70 stalls

Antiques Fair
The Willerby Manor
Hull
East Yorkshire
Abbey Antiques Fairs:
01482 445785
Monthly

Antiques Fair
The Village Hall
Pooley Bridge
Cumbria
Albany Fairs: 0191 584 2934
Monthly

Antiques Fair
The Town Hall
Bellingham
Northumberland
Albany Fairs: 0191 584 2934
Annually (August)

Antiques Fair
The Leaplish Waterside Park
Northumberland
Albany Fairs: 0191 584 2934
Annually (August)

Antiques Fair
The Scarth Hall
Staindrop
County Durham
Albany Fairs: 0191 584 2934
Annually (September)

Antiques Fair
The Community Centre
Lanchester
County Durham
Albany Fairs: 0191 584 2934
Annually (November)

The Cheshire Summer Antiques & 20th Century Fair
Tatton Park
Knutsford
Cheshire
Bailey Fairs: 01277 214699
Annually (July)

The Cheshire Antiques Fair
Tatton Park
Knutsford
Cheshire
Bailey Fairs: 01277 214699
Three times a year (January, March and September) – 54 stalls

The Ilkley Antiques Fair
The Kings Hall & Winter Gardens
Ilkley
West Yorkshire
Bailey Fairs: 01277 214699
Annually (August)

The Cumbria Antiques Fair
The Holker Hall
Cark in Carmel
Nr Grange Over Sands
Cumbria
Bailey Fairs: 01277 214699
Annually (November)

**The Lancashire Christmas
Antiques Fair**
Hoghton Tower
Hoghton
Nr Preston
Lancashire
Bailey Fairs: 01277 214699
Annually (December)

**Monmouthshire County
Antiques & Collectors' Fair**
The Market Hall
Monmouth
Contact: 01873 735811
*Bi-annually (February and June) –
over 60 stalls plus flea market*

Antiques Fair
The Village Hall
Cartmel
Cumbria
Cartmel Antiques Fairs:
01253 396209
Monthly

Antiques & Collectors' Fair
The Kendal Leisure Centre
Kendal
Cumbria
Colin Caygill Events:
0191 261 9632
Annually (September)

Antiques & Collectors' Fair
The Wentworth Leisure Centre
Hexham
Northumberland
Colin Caygill Events:
0191 261 9632
*Three times a year (July, August
and September)*

Antiques & Collectors' Fair
The Riverside Leisure Centre
Morpeth
Northumberland
Colin Caygill Events:
0191 261 9632
Annually (August)

Antiques & Collectors' Fair
The International Stadium
Gateshead
Tyne & Wear
Colin Caygill Events:
0191 261 9632
Bi-annually (July and September)

Antiques & Collectors' Fair
The Graham Sports Centre
Durham University
County Durham
Colin Caygill Events:
0191 261 9632
Bi-annually (July and September)

Antiques & Collectors' Fair
The Sands Centre
City of Carlisle
Cumbria
Colin Caygill Events:
0191 261 9632
Bi-annually (July and September)

Antiques & Collectors' Fair
Skirsgill Hall
P.F.K. Mart
Penrith
Cumbria
Colin Caygill Events:
0191 261 9632

Antiques & Collectors' Fair
The County Hall
Durham City
County Durham
Colin Caygill Events:
0191 261 9632
Annually (July)

**The Cheshire Country
Antiques Fair**
The Arley Hall
Nr Knutsford
Cheshire
Colin Caygill Events:
0191 261 9632
Annually (October)

The Duncombe Park
Antiques Fair
Nr Helimsley
North Yorkshire
Galloway Antiques Fairs:
01423 522122
Annually (November)

Antiques Fair
Ripley Castle
Ripley
Nr Harrogate
North Yorkshire
Galloway Antiques Fairs:
01423 522122
Annually (July)

Antiques Fair
The Naworth Castle
Brampton
Cumbria
Galloway Antiques Fairs:
01423 522122
Annually (August)

Antiques Fair
The Old Swan Hotel
Harrogate
North Yorkshire
Galloway Antiques Fairs:
01423 522122
Annually (September)

Antiques Fair
The Stonyhurst College
Clitheroe
Lancashire
Galloway Antiques Fairs:
01423 522122
Annually (October)

Antiques Fair
Blackpool Winter Gardens
Blackpool
Lancashire
Hoyles Promotions: 01253 782828
Monthly
The Christmas Fair is at the
Empress Ballroom in Blackpool

Antiques & Collectors' Fair
Civic Hall
Nantwich
Cheshire
Stacie Kutler Fairs: 01270 624288
Monthly

Antiques & Collectors'
Jamboree
Civic Hall
Nantwich
Cheshire
Stacie Kutler Fairs: 01270 624288
Bi-annually (August and
December)

Antiques & Collectors' Fair
The Plumley Village Hall
Near Knutsford
Cheshire
N&B Fairs: 01565 722144
Most months

The Chester Antiques
& Fine Art Fair
The County Grandstand
Chester Racecourse
Chester
Cheshire
Penman Fairs: 01444 482514
Annually (October) – 50 stalls

Anthony Porter's Flea market
York Racecourse Grandstand
Pontrefract
West Yorkshire
Contact: 01977 644933
Eight times a year – 120 stalls

Antiques Fair
Exhibition Hall
Charnock Richard
Chorley
Lancashire
Unicorn Fairs: 0161 773 7001
Weekly (every Sunday) – 180 stalls

Antiques & Collectors' Fair
The Exhibition Halls
Park Hall
Charnock Richard
Lancashire
Unicorn Fairs: 0161 773 7001
Weekly

**The Harrogate Antiques
& Fine Art Fair**
The Harrogate International
Centre
Harrogate
North Yorkshire
Contact: 01823 323 363
Annually (October)

SCOTLAND

Antiques Fair
The Town Hall
St Andrews
Fife
Albany Fairs: 0191 584 2934
*Bi-annually (August and
September)*

Antiques Fair
The Town Hall
Moffat
Dumfriesshire
Monthly

**The Gleneagles Antiques
& Fine Arts Fair**
The Gleneagles Hotel
Auchterarder
Perthshire
Bailey Fairs: 01277 214699
Annually (December)

Antiques for Everyone
Scottish Exhibition & Conference
Centre
Glasgow
Centre Exhibitions: 0121 767
2665
Annually (August)

Antiques Fair
Scone Palace
Perth
Galloway Antiques Fairs:
01423 522122
Annually (November)

WALES

Chirk Giant Sunday Market
Chirk Castle
Chirk
Digwyddiadan Cwmpas Events:
01691 778095
*Weekly (every Sunday during April
to September)*

Antiques Fair
The Heath Park Sports Centre
Heath
Cardiff
South Glamorgan
David Robinson Fairs:
01222 620 520
Bi-annually (July and October)

Antiques & Collectors' Fair
The Copthorne Hotel
Culverhouse Cross
Cardiff
South Glamorgan
David Robinson Fairs:
01222 620 520
*Bi-annually (August and
November)*

Antiques Fair
The Village Hotel
Coryton
Cardiff
David Robinson Fairs:
01222 620 520
*Bi-annually (September and
November)*

Antiques Fair
The Rest Bay
Porthcawl
Mid Glamorgan
David Robinson Fairs:
01222 620 520
Annually (November)

Antiques & Collectors' Fair
Sophia Gardens
Cardiff
Towy Antiques Fairs:
01267 236569
Bi-annually (April and September)
– 100 stalls

Antiques & Collectors' Fair
The United Counties
Showground
Carmarthen
Towy Antiques Fairs:
01267 236 569
Four times a year (March, May,
September and December) – 180
stalls
The biggest antiques and collectors'
fair in Wales

Antiques Fair
The Brangwyn Hall
Guildhall
Swansea
Towy Antiques Fairs:
01267 236 569
Bi-annually (July and October)

Antiques & Collectors' Fair
The City Hall
Cathays Park
Cardiff
Towy Antiques Fairs:
01267 236 569
Bi-annually (September and
October)

THE ANTIQUES YEAR

There are shows, fairs and markets
happening all over the country all
the time but the calendar below
should provide a general guide to
the bigger events of the antiques
year. Much of the information is
repeated from the Fairs and Markets
section but broken down into
months so you can plan ahead.

JANUARY

The Cheshire Antiques Fair
Tatton Park
Knutsford
Cheshire
Bailey Fairs: 01277 214699

**The LAPADA (London
& Provincial Antique Dealers'
Association) Fair**
National Exhibition Centre
Birmingham
West Midlands
Centre Exhibitions:
0121 767 2665

**The Decorative Antiques
& Textiles Fair**
The Marquee
Riverside Terrace
Battersea Park
SW11
Heritage Fairs: 020 7624 5173

**The Kensington Antiques
& Fine Art Fair**
Kensington Town Hall
Hornton Street
London
W8
Penman Fairs: 01444 482514

FEBRUARY

Antiques Fair
The Big Venue
Luton Sports Centre
Luton
Hertfordshire
A1 Fairs: 01702 203503

Antiques Fair
The Old Swan Hotel
Harrogate
North Yorkshire
Abbey Antiques Fairs:
01482 445785

**The Spring Olympia Fine Art
& Antiques Fair**
Olympia Exhibition Centre
Hammersmith Road
London
W14
Clarion Events Ltd:
020 7370 8188

Antiques Fair
The Cresset
Bretton Centre
Peterborough
Cambridgeshire
Bob Evans Fairs: 01733 265705

**The Milton Keynes
Antiques Fair**
The Middleton Hall
Central Milton Keynes
Regional Shopping Centre
Buckinghamshire
E. W. Services: 01933 225674

The Luton Antiques Fair
The Putteridge Bury House
Luton
Hertfordshire
Contact: 01234 381 701

**Monmouthshire County
Antiques & Collectors' Fair**
The Market Hall
Monmouth
Contact: 01873 735811

The Petersfield Antiques Fair
The Festival Hall
Petersfield
Hampshire
Penman Fairs: 01444 482514

South East Antiques Fairs
Donnington Manor Hotel
London Road
Dunton Green
Sevenoaks
Kent
South East Fairs: 01892 653379

**London Art Deco
& Modernist Fair**
The Canons
Madeira Road
Mitcham
Surrey
Contact: 020 8663 3323

MARCH

Antiques & Collectors' Fair
The Goodwood Racecourse
Near Chichester
West Sussex
Antiques & Collectors World:
01737 812989

**The Hertfordshire Antiques
& Fine Art Fair**
Hatfield House
The Goscoyne Cecil Estate
Hatfield Park
Hertfordshire
Bailey Fairs: 01277 214699

**The BADA (British Antique
Dealers' Association) Antiques
& Fine Art Fair**
The Duke of York's Headquarters
King's Road
Chelsea
London
SW3
BADA: 020 7589 6108

The Cheshire Antiques Fair
Tatton Park
Knutsford
Cheshire
Bailey Fairs: 01277 214699

Antiques & Collectors' Fair
The Canons Leisure Centre
Madeira Road
Mitcham
Big Surrey Fairs: 020 8390 1230

Antiques & Collectors' Fair
The Tolworth Recreation Centre
A3 Kingston Bypass
Surrey
Big Surrey Fairs Ltd:
020 8390 1230

**The Malvern Antiques
& Collectors' Fair**
Three Counties Showground
Malvern
Worcestershire
DMG Antiques Fairs:
01636 702326

The Mid-Beds Antiques Fair
Silsoe College and Conference
Centre
Silsoe
Bedfordshire
Contact: 01234 381701

The Chelsea Antiques Fair
Chelsea Old Town Hall
Chelsea
London
SW3
Penman: 01444 482514

South East Antiques Fairs
Donnington Manor Hotel
London Road
Dunton Green
Sevenoaks
Kent
South East Fairs: 01892 653379

Antiques & Collectors' Fair
The United Counties
Showground
Carmarthen
Towy Antiques Fairs:
01267 236 569

APRIL

The London Arms Fair
The Royal National Hotel
Bedford Way
WC1
Arms Fair Ltd: 020 8539 5278

Antiques for Everyone
Hall 5
The National Exhibition Centre
Birmingham
West Midlands
Centre Exhibitions:
0121 767 2760

**The South Cotswold
Antiques Fair**
Westonbirt School
Tetbury
Gloucestershire
Cooper Antiques Fairs:
01249 661111

**The Decorative Antiques
& Textiles Fair**
The Marquee
Riverside Terrace
Battersea Park
SW11
Heritage Fairs: 020 7624 5173

The Chelsea Art Fair
Chelsea Old Town Hall
King's Road
Chelsea
London
SW3
Penman: 01444 482514

MAY

Antiques & Collectors' Fair
The United Counties
Showground
Carmarthen
Towy Antiques Fairs:
01267 236 569

JUNE

**The Summer Olympia Fine
Art & Antiques Fair**
Olympia Exhibition Centre
Hammersmith Rd
London
W14
Clarion Events Ltd:
020 7370 8188

The Ephemera Society Fair
The Hotel Russell
Russell Square
WC1
The Ephemera Society:
01923 829079

**The Grosvenor House Art
& Antiques Fair**
Grosvenor House
Park Lane
London
W1
Contact: 020 7589 4128

**Monmouthshire County
Antiques & Collectors' Fair**
The Market Hall
Monmouth
Contact: 01873 735811

The Petersfield Antiques Fair
The Festival Hall
Petersfield
Hants
Penman Fairs: 01444 482514

South East Antiques Fairs
Winston Manor Hotel
Beacon Road
Crowborough
East Sussex
South East Fairs: 01892 653379

July

Antiques & Collectors' Fair
The International Arena
Wood Green Animal Shelter
London Road
Godmanchester
Huntingdon
Cambridgeshire
Aztec Fairs: 01702 233123

**The Cheshire Summer
Antiques & 20th Century Fair**
Tatton Park
Knutsford
Cheshire
Bailey Fairs: 01277 214699

Antiques & Collectors' Fair
The Leisure Centre
Hurst Road
Walton-on-Thames
Surrey
Big Surrey Fairs Ltd: 020 8390
1230

Antiques & Collectors' Fair
The Wentworth Leisure Centre
Hexham
Northumberland
Colin Caygill Events:
0191 261 9632

Antiques & Collectors' Fair
The International Stadium
Gateshead
Tyne & Wear
Colin Caygill Events:
0191 261 9632

Antiques & Collectors' Fair
The Graham Sports Centre
Durham University
County Durham
Colin Caygill Events:
0191 261 9632

Antiques & Collectors' Fair
The Sands Centre
City of Carlisle
Cumbria
Colin Caygill Events:
0191 261 9632

Antiques & Collectors' Fair
The County Hall
Durham City
County Durham
Colin Caygill Events:
0191 261 9632

**The Annual Snape
Antiques Fair**
Snape
Suffolk
Cooper Antiques Fairs:
01249 661111

Antiques & Collectors' Fair
The Parklands Leisure Centre
Oadby
Leicestershire
County Fairs: 0700 0432477

**The North Cotswold
Antiques Fair**
Stanway House
Nr Winchcombe
Gloucestershire
Cooper Antiques Fairs:
01249 661111

Antiques & Collectors' Fair
The Essex Country Showground
Chelmsford
Essex
DMG Antiques Fairs:
01636 702326

Antiques & Collectors' Fair
Hall 3
The Exhibition Centre
Empire Way
Wembley
DMG Antiques Fairs:
01636 702326

Antiques Fair
Cranleigh School
Cranleigh
Surrey
Galloway Antiques Fairs:
01423 522122

Antiques Fair
Ripley Castle
Ripley
Nr Harrogate
North Yorkshire
Galloway Antiques Fairs:
01423 522122

Antiques & Collectors' Fair
Kingston Maurward House
The Dorset College of Agriculture
& Horticulture
Dorchester
Dorset
Grandma's Attic Antiques Fairs:
01590 677687

Antiques & Collectors' Fair
The Jubilee Hall
Chagford
Devon
Sheila Hyson Fairs:
01647 231 459

The Decorative Arts Fair
Fulham Town Hall
Fulham Broadway
SW6
P & A Antiques: 020 8543 5075

Antiques & Collectors' Fair
The Silverstone Motor Racing
Circuit
Silverstone
Northamptonshire
R&S Fairs: 01702 345222

Antiques Fair
The Heath Park Sports Centre
Heath
Cardiff
South Glamorgan
David Robinson Fairs:
01222 620 520

Antiques & Collectors' Fair
The Woking Leisure Centre
Kingfield Road
Woking
Surrey
Take Five Fairs: 020 8894 0218

Antiques & Collectors' Fair
The Rainbow Centre
East Street
Epsom
Surrey
Take Five Fairs: 020 8894 0218

Antiques Fair
The Brangwyn Hall
Guildhall
Swansea
Towy Antiques Fairs:
01267 236 569

August

Antiques Fair
The Town Hall
Bellingham
Northumberland
Albany Fairs: 0191 584 2934

Antiques Fair
The Leaplish Waterside Park
Northumberland
Albany Fairs: 0191 584 2934

Antiques Fair
The Town Hall
St Andrews
Fife
Albany Fairs: 0191 584 2934

Antiques & Collectors' Fair
The Brentwood Centre
Doddinghurst Road
Brentwood
Essex
Aztec Fairs: 01702 233123

Antiques & Collectors' Fair
The Norfolk Showground
New Costessey
Norfolk
Aztec Fairs: 01702 233123

Antiques & Collectors' Fair
The Suffolk Showground
Bucklesham Road
Ipswich
Suffolk
Aztec Fairs: 01702 233123

The Ilkley Antiques Fair
The Kings Hall & Winter
Gardnes
Ilkley
West Yorkshire
Bailey Fairs: 01277 214699

Antiques & Collectors' Fair
The Wentworth Leisure Centre
Hexham
Northumberland
Colin Caygill Events:
0191 261 9632

Antiques & Collectors' Fair
The Riverside Leisure Centre
Morpeth
Northumberland
Colin Caygill Events:
0191 261 9632

Antiques for Everyone
Hall 5
The National Exhibition Centre
Birmingham
West Midlands
Centre Exhibitions:
0121 767 2760

Antiques for Everyone
Scottish Exhibition & Conference
Centre
Glasgow
Centre Exhibitions:
0121 767 2760

**The South Cotswold
Antiques Fair**
Westonbirt School
Tetbury
Gloucestershire
Cooper Antiques Fairs:
01249 661111

Antiques & Collectors' Fair
The Community College
Desford
Leicestershire
County Fairs: 0700 0432477

Antiques & Collectors' Fair
The School
Uppingham
Leicestershire
County Fairs: 0700 0432477

Art & Collectors' Fair
The Newmarket Racecourse
Newmarket
Suffolk
DMG Antiques Fairs:
01636 702326

Antiques Fair
The Wrekin College
Wellington
Shropshire
Galloway Antiques Fairs:
01423 522122

Antiques Fair
The Naworth Castle
Brampton
Cumbria
Galloway Antiques Fairs:
01423 522122

The Allendale Centre
Hanham Road
Wimborne
Dorset
Grandma's Attic Antiques Fairs:
01590 677687

Antiques Fair
The River Park Leisure Centre
Gordon Road
Winchester
Hampshire
Magnum Antiques Fairs:
01491 681009

Antiques & Collectors' Fair
The Cheltenham Racecourse
Cheltenham
Gloucestershire
Melba Fairs: 01934 412923

Antiques Fair
The Bellhouse Hotel
Oxford Road
Beaconsfield
Buckinghamshire
Midas Fairs: 01494 674170

Antiques Fair
The Brighton Centre
Kings Road
Brighton
Sussex
Shirley Mostyn Fairs:
01903 752961

**The Kensington Antiques
& Fine Art Fair**
Kensington Town Hall
Hornton St
London
W8
Penman Fairs: 01444 482514

Antiques & Collectors' Fair
The Warwick University
Art Centre
Central Campus
Gibbet Hill Road
Coventry
West Midlands
Profile Promotions:
0121 449 4246

Antiques & Collectors' Fair
The Suffolk Showground
Bucklesham Road
Ipswich
Suffolk
R&S Fairs: 01702 345222

Antiques Fair
The Southend Bandstand
Clifftown Parade
Southend on Sea
Essex
Ridgeway Fairs: 01702 710383

Antiques Fair
The Mill Hall
Rayleigh
Essex
Ridgeway Fairs: 01702 710383

Antiques Fair
The Marks Hall Estate
Coggeshall
Essex
Ridgeway Fairs: 01702 710383

Antiques & Collectors' Fair
The Copthorne Hotel
Culverhouse Cross
Cardiff
South Glamorgan
David Robinson Fairs:
01222 620 520

SEPTEMBER

Antiques Fair
The Scarth Hall
Staindrop
County Durham
Albany Fairs: 0191 584 2934

Antiques Fair
The Town Hall
St Andrews
Fife
Albany Fairs: 0191 584 2934

The London Arms Fair
The Royal National Hotel
Bedford Way
WC1
Arms Fair Ltd: 020 8539 5278

Antiques & Collectors' Fair
The Riverside Leisure Centre
Victoria Road
Chelmsford
Essex
Aztec Fairs: 01702 233123

**The Cheshire Fine Arts
& Antiques Fair**
Tatton Park
Knutsford
Cheshire
Bailey Fairs: 01277 214699

Antiques & Collectors' Fair
The Leisure Centre
Hurst Road
Walton-on-Thames
Surrey
Big Surrey Fairs Ltd:
020 8390 1230

Antiques & Collectors' Fair
The Kendal Leisure Centre
Kendal
Cumbria
Colin Caygill Events:
0191 261 9632

Antiques & Collectors' Fair
The Wentworth Leisure Centre
Hexham
Northumberland
Colin Caygill Events:
0191 261 9632

Antiques & Collectors' Fair
The International Stadium
Gateshead
Tyne & Wear
Colin Caygill Events:
0191 261 9632

Antiques & Collectors' Fair
The Graham Sports Centre
Durham University
County Durham
Colin Caygill Events:
0191 261 9632

Antiques & Collectors' Fair
The Salisbury Leisure Centre
The Butts
Hulse Road
Salisbury
Wiltshire
Cooper Antiques Fairs:
01249 661111

Antiques & Collectors' Fair
The Town Hall
Loughborough
Leicestershire
County Fairs: 0700 0432477

Antiques & Collectors' Fair
The Village Hall
Newtown Linford
Leicestershire
County Fairs: 0700 0432477

Antiques & Collectors' Fair
The College
Countersthorpe
Leicestershire
County Fairs: 0700 0432477

Antiques & Collectors' Fair
The Village Hall
Gaddesby
Leicestershire
County Fairs: 0700 0432477

Antique & Collectors' Fair
The Essex Country Showground
Chelmsford
Essex
DMG Antiques Fairs:
01636 702326

**The Milton Keynes
Antiques Fair**
The Middleton Hall
Central Milton Keynes
Regional Shopping Centre
Buckinghamshire
E. W. Services: 01933 225674

Antiques Fair
Hatfield Galleria Retail Outlet
Centre
Comet Way
Hatfield
Hertfordshire
E. W. Services Antiques Fairs:
01933 225674

Antiques Fair
The Haggley Hall
Stourbridge
Worcestershire
Galloway Antiques Fairs:
01423 522122

Antiques Fair
The Old Swan Hotel
Harrogate
North Yorkshire
Galloway Antiques Fairs:
01423 522122

Antiques & Collectors' Fair
Kingston Maurward House
The Dorset College of Agriculture
& Horticulture
Dorchester
Dorset
Grandma's Attic Antiques Fairs:
01590 677687

Antiques & Collectors' Fair
St Thomas' Church Hall
Lymington
Hampshire
Grandma's Attic Fairs:
01590 677687

**The London International
Antique & Artist Dolls, Toys,
Miniature & Teddy Bear Fair**
Kensington Town Hall
Exhibition & Conference Facility
Hornton Street
London
W8
Grannies Goodies:
020 8693 5432

Antiques Fair
The Southend Tennis & Leisure
Centre
Eastern Avenue
Southend
Essex
Hallmark Antiques Fairs Ltd:
01702 710383

Antiques Fair
The Cressing Temple Barns
Witham
Essex
Hallmark Antiques Fairs Ltd:
01702 710383

**The Decorative Antiques
& Textiles Fair**
The Marquee
Riverside Terrace
Battersea Park
SW11
Heritage Fairs: 020 7624 5173

**The Woolverstone Fine Art
& Antiques Fair**
Ipswich High School for Girls
Nr Ipswich
Suffolk
Lomax Antiques Fairs:
01603 737631

Antiques & Collectors' Fair
The Royal Chace Hotel
Queens Banqueting Suite
The Ridgeway
Enfield
Middlesex
M & S Enterprises:
020 8440 2330

The Chelsea Antiques Fair
Chelsea Old Town Hall
King's Rd
Chelsea
London
SW3
Penman Fairs: 01444 482514

The Petersfield Antiques Fair
The Festival Hall
Petersfield
Hants
Penman Fairs: 01444 482514

Antiques & Collectors' Fair
The Royal Spa Centre
Newbold Terrace
Leamington Spa
Warwickshire
Profile Promotions:
0121 449 4246

Antiques & Collectors' Fair
The Leisure World
Cowdray Avenue
Colchester
Essex
R&S Fairs: 01702 345222

Antiques Fair
The Village Hotel
Coryton
Cardiff
David Robinson Fairs:
01222 620 520

Antiques & Collectors' Fair
The City Hall
Cathays Park
Cardiff
Towy Antiques Fairs:
01267 236 569

OCTOBER

Antiques & Collectors' Fair
The Suffolk Showground
Bucklesham Road
Ipswich
Suffolk
Aztec Fairs: 01702 233123

**The Warwickshire Antiques
& Fine Art Fair**
Ragley Hall
Alcester
Warwickshire
Bailey Fairs: 01277 214699

**The Buxton Autumn Fine Art
& Antiques Fair**
The Pavilion Gardens
Buxton
Derbyshire
Bailey Fairs: 01277 214699

**The Cheshire Country
Antiques Fair**
The Arley Hall
Nr Knutsford
Cheshire
Colin Caygill Events:
0191 261 9632

**The LAPADA (London
& Provincial Antique Dealers'
Association) Fair**
The Commonwealth Institute
Kensington High Street
London
W8
Centre Exhibitions:
0121 767 2665

The Great Antiques Fair
Earls Court Exhibition Centre
Earls Court
London
SW5
Clarion Events Ltd:
020 7370 8188

Antiques & Collectors' Fair
The Sketchley Grange Hotel
Hinckley
Leicestershire
County Fairs: 0700 0432477

Antiques & Collectors' Fair
The Leisure Centre
Enderby
Leicestershire
County Fairs: 0700 0432477

Antiques & Collectors' Fair
The Stage Hotel
Wigston Fields
Leicestershire
County Fairs: 0700 0432477

The Surrey Antiques Fair
Civic Hall
Guildford
Surrey
Cultural Exhibitions Ltd:
01483 422562

Antiques & Collectors' Fair
The Exhibition Centre
Warwick
Warwickshire
DMG Antiques Fairs:
01636 702326

Antiques & Collectors' Fair
Hall 3
The Exhibition Centre
Empire Way
Wembley
London
DMG Antiques Fairs:
01636 702326

Antiques & Collectors' Fair
The Essex Country Showground
Chelmsford
Essex
DMG Antique Fairs:
01636 702326

The Luton Antiques Fair
The Putteridge Bury House
Luton
Hertfordshire
Contact: 01234 381 701

Antiques Fair
Seaford College
Near Petworth
West Sussex
Galloway Antiques Fairs:
01423 522122

Antiques Fair
The Haggley Hall
Stourbridge
Worcestershire
Galloway Antiques Fairs:
01423 522122

Antiques Fair
Deene Park
Corby
Northamptonshire
Galloway Antiques Fairs:
01423 522122

Antiques Fair
The Stonyhurst College
Clitheroe
Lancashire
Galloway Antiques Fairs:
01423 522122

Antiques & Collectors' Fair
The Potters Heron Hotel
Hampshire
Grandma's Attic Fairs:
01590 677687

Antiques & Collectors' Fair
Botleigh Grange
Botley Hedge End
Hampshire
Grandma's Attic Fairs:
01590 677687

The Allendale Centre
Hanham Road
Wimborne
Dorset
Grandma's Attic Antiques Fairs:
01590 677687

Antiques Fair
The Courage Hall
Brentwood School
Middleton Hall Lane
Brentwood
Essex
Hallmark Antiques Fairs Ltd:
01702 71038

Antiques Fair
The Southend Cliffs Pavilion
Station Road
Westcliff on Sea
Essex
Hallmark Antiques Fairs Ltd:
01702 71038

The Harrogate Antiques & Fine Art Fair
The Harrogate International Centre
Harrogate
North Yorkshire
Contact: 01823 323 363

Antiques & Collectors' Fair
The Jubilee Hall
Chagford
Devon
Sheila Hyson Fairs:
01647 231 459

Antiques Fair
The Lister Harpur Suite
Corn Exchange Complex
Bedford
Bedfordshire
Janba Fairs: 01945 870160

The East Anglian Antiques Dealers' Fair
The Langley Park School
Loddon
Norfolk
Lomax Antiques Fairs:
01603 737631

Antiques & Collectors' Fair
The Royal Chace Hotel
Queens Banqueting Suite
The Ridgeway
Enfield
Middlesex
M & S Enterprises:
020 8440 2330

Antiques Fair
The River Park Leisure Centre
Gordon Road
Winchester
Hampshire
Magnum Antiques Fairs:
01491 681009

Antiques Fair
The Brighton Centre
Kings Road
Brighton
Sussex
Shirley Mostyn Fairs:
01903 752961

**The Chester Antiques
& Fine Art Fair**
The County Grandstand
Chester Racecourse
Chester
Cheshire
Penman Fairs: 01444 482514

Antiques & Collectors' Fair
The Suffolk Showground
Bucklesham Road
Ipswich
Suffolk
R&S Fairs: 01702 345222

Antiques & Collectors' Fair
The Hickstead Showground
London Road
Hickstead
West Sussex
R&S Fairs: 01702 345222

Antiques & Collectors' Fair
The Dolphin Leisure Centre
Pasture Hill Road
Haywards Heath
West Sussex
R&S Fairs: 01702 345222

Antiques & Collectors' Fair
The Sir James Hawkey Hall
Broadmead Road
Woodford Green
Essex
R&S Fairs: 01702 345222

Antiques & Collectors' Fair
The Sports Centre
Harrow Lodge Park
Hornchurch Road
Hornchurch
Essex
R&S Fairs: 01702 345222

Antiques Fair
Keys Hall
Eagle Way
Great Warley
Nr Brentwood
Essex
Ridgeway Fairs: 01702 710383

Antiques Fair
The Thurrock Civic Hall
Blackshott's Lane
Grays
Essex
Ridgeway Fairs: 01702 710383

Antiques Fair
The Marconi Sports & Social
Club
Beehive Lane
Great Baddow
Chelmsford
Essex
Ridgeway Fairs: 01702 710383

Antiques Fair
The Heath Park Sports Centre
Heath
Cardiff
South Glamorgan
David Robinson Fairs:
01222 620 520

Antiques & Collectors' Fair
The United Counties
Showground
Carmarthen
Towy Antiques Fairs:
01267 236 569

Antiques Fair
The Shuttleworth Mansion
Old Warren Park
Biggleswade
Bedfordshire
Graham Turner Antiques Fairs:
01473 658224

South East Antiques Fairs
Donnington Manor Hotel
London Road
Dunton Green
Sevenoaks
Kent
South East Fairs: 01892 653379

Antiques & Collectors' Fair
The City Hall
Cathays Park
Cardiff
Towy Antiques Fairs:
01267 236 569

Antiques Fair
The Brangwyn Hall
Guildhall
Swansea
Towy Antiques Fairs:
01267 236 569

Antiques Fairs
The Sandown Exhibition Centre
Sandown Park Racecourse
Esher
Surrey
Wonder Whistle Enterprises:
020 7249 4050

November

Antiques Fair
The Community Centre
Lanchester
County Durham
Albany Fairs: 0191 584 2934

Antiques & Collectors' Fair
The Brentwood Centre
Doddinghurst Road
Brentwood
Essex
Aztec Fairs: 01702 233123

Antiques & Collectors' Fair
The Norfolk Showground
New Costessey
Norfolk
Aztec Fairs: 01702 233123

Antiques & Collectors' Fair
The Riverside Leisure Centre
Victoria Road
Chelmsford
Essex
Aztec Fairs: 01702 233123

**The Hertfordshire Antiques &
Fine Art Fair**
Hatfield House
The Goscoyne Cecil Estate
Hatfield Park
Hertfordshire
Bailey Fairs: 01277 214699

The Cumbria Antiques Fair
The Holker Hall
Cark in Carmel
Nr Grange Over Sands
Cumbria
Bailey Fairs: 01277 214699

**The Nottinghamshire Arts &
Antiques Fair**
The Thoresby Park
Nr Ollerton
Notts
Bailey Fairs: 01277 214699

Antiques & Collectors' Fair
The Town Hall
Clare
Suffolk
Best of Fairs: 01787 280306

The Winter Olympia Fine Art & Antiques Fair
The National Hall
Olympia Exhibition Centre
Hammersmith Road
London
W14
Clarion Events Ltd:
020 7370 8188

Antiques for Everyone
Hall 5
The National Exhibition Centre
Birmingham
West Midlands
Centre Exhibitions:
0121 767 2760

Moreton Hall Antiques Fair
Moreton Hall
Warwickshire College of Agriculture
Moreton Morrell
Warwickshire
Cooper Antiques Fairs:
01249 661111

Antiques & Collectors' Fair
The Town Hall
Loughborough
Leicestershire
County Fairs: 0700 0432477

Antiques & Collectors' Fair
The Community College
Desford
Leicestershire
County Fairs: 0700 0432477

Antiques & Collectors' Fair
The Leicester City Football Club
Filbert Street
Leicester
Leicestershire
County Fairs: 0700 0432477

Antiques & Collectors' Fair
The Rockingham Forest Hotel
Corby
Leicestershire
County Fairs: 0700 0432477

Antiques & Collectors' Fair
The Newmarket Racecourse
Newmarket
Suffolk
DMG Antiques Fairs:
01636 702326

Antiques & Collectors' Fair
The National Agricultural Centre
Stoneleigh
Warwickshire
DMG Antiques Fairs:
01636 702326

Antiques Fair
Hatfield Galleria Retail Outlet
Centre
Comet Way
Hatfield
Hertfordshire
E. W. Services Antiques Fairs:
01933 225674

The Duncombe Park Antiques Fair
Nr Helimsley
North Yorkshire
Galloway Antiques Fairs:
01423 522122

Antiques Fair
Scone Palace
Perth
Galloway Antiques Fairs:
01423 522122

The London International Antique & Artist Dolls, Toys, Miniature & Teddy Bear Fair
Kensington Town Hall
Exhibition & Conference Facility
Hornton Street
W8
Grannies Goodies:
020 8693 5432

Antiques & Collectors' Fair
St Thomas' Church Hall
Lymington
Hampshire
Grandma's Attic Fairs:
01590 677687

Antiques & Collectors' Fair
The Littledown Centre
Castle Lane
North East of Bournemouth
Dorset
Grandma's Attic Antiques Fairs:
01590 677687

Antiques & Collectors' Fair
Kingston Maurward House
The Dorset College of Agriculture
& Horticulture
Dorchester
Dorset
Grandma's Attic Antiques Fairs:
01590 677687

Antique & Collectors' Fair
The Royal Chace Hotel
Queens Banqueting Suite
The Ridgeway
Enfield
Middlesex
M & S Enterprises:
020 8440 2330

The Mid-Beds Antiques Fair
Silsoe College and Conference
Centre
Silsoe
Bedfordshire
Contact: 01234 381701

Antiques & Collectors' Fair
The Royal Spa Centre
Newbold Terrace
Leamington Spa
Warwickshire
Profile Promotions:
0121 449 4246

Antiques Fair
The Mill Hall
Rayleigh
Essex
Ridgeway Fairs: 01702 710383

Antiques & Collectors' Fair
The Copthorne Hotel
Culverhouse Cross
Cardiff
South Glamorgan
David Robinson Fairs:
01222 620 520

Antiques Fair
The Village Hotel
Coryton
Cardiff
David Robinson Fairs:
01222 620 520

Antiques Fair
The Rest Bay
Porthcawl
Mid Glamorgan
David Robinson Fairs:
01222 620 520

South East Antiques Fairs
Winston Manor Hotel
Beacon Road
Crowborough
East Sussex
South East Fairs: 01892 653379

Antiques Fairs
The Sandown Exhibition Centre
Sandown Park Racecourse
Esher
Surrey
Wonder Whistle Enterprises:
020 7249 4050

DECEMBER

Antiques & Collectors' Fair
The International Arena
Wood Green Animal Shelter
London Road
Godmanchester
Huntingdon
Cambridgeshire
Aztec Fairs: 01702 233123

**The Gleneagles Antiques
& Fine Arts Fair**
The Gleneagles Hotel
Auchterarder
Perthshire
Bailey Fairs: 01277 214699

**The Lancashire Christmas
Antiques Fair**
Hoghton Tower
Hoghton
Nr Preston
Lancashire
Bailey Fairs: 01277 214699

Antiques & Collectors' Fair
The Salisbury Leisure Centre
The Butts
Hulse Road
Salisbury
Wiltshire
Cooper Antiques Fairs:
01249 661111

**The South Cotswold
Antiques Fair**
Westonbirt School
Tetbury
Gloucestershire
Cooper Antiques Fairs:
01249 661111

Antiques & Collectors' Fair
The Village Hall
Newtown Linford
Leicestershire
County Fairs: 0700 0432477

Antiques & Collectors' Fair
The Parklands Leisure Centre
Oadby
Leicestershire
County Fairs: 0700 0432477

Antiques & Collectors' Fair
The Exhibition Centre
Warwick
Warwickshire
DMG Antiques Fairs:
01636 702326

The Ephemera Society Fair
The Hotel Russell
Russell Square
WC1
The Ephemera Society:
01923 829079

Antiques Fair
The Powerham Castle
Exeter
Devon
Galloway Antiques Fairs:
01423 522122

The Allendale Centre
Hanham Road
Wimborne
Dorset
Grandma's Attic Antiques Fairs:
01590 677687

Antiques & Collectors' Fair
The Potters Heron Hotel
Hampshire
Grandma's Attic Fairs:
01590 677687

Antiques & Collectors' Fair
The Jubilee Hall
Chagford
Devon
Sheila Hyson Fairs:
01647 231 459

Antiques Fair
The Lister Harpur Suite
Corn Exchange Complex
Bedford
Bedfordshire
Janba Fairs: 01945 870160

Antiques & Collectors' Fair
The Sports Centre
Harrow Lodge Park
Hornchurch Road
Hornchurch
Essex
R&S Fairs: 01702 345222

Antiques Fair
Keys Hall
Eagle Way
Great Warley
Nr Brentwood
Essex
Ridgeway Fairs: 01702 710383

Antiques & Collectors' Fair
The United Counties
Showground
Carmarthen
Towy Antiques Fairs:
01267 236 569